MW01077637

MERCILESS
WATERS

"Erotic and sensually developed. Lush with vibrant characters and unashamed in its horror and honesty, *Merciless Waters* is a powerful rush from cover to cover."
—C.S. Humble, author of the *Black Wells* series

"Lush and imaginative, tense and atmospheric, *Merciless Waters* is a vengeful fever dream drowned in saltwater."
—Rachel Harrison, national bestselling author of *Cackle* and *Such Sharp Teeth*

"Batten down the hatches because Rae Knowles will drag you to the briny depths with this wild, immersive tale of seafaring adventure, ancient myth, grim revenge, and salty desire. These women buccaneers will hook you!"
—Tim McGregor, author of *Lure*

A worthy follow-up to *The Stradivarius*, Rae Knowles' *Merciless Waters* is a visceral, sexy, and sweetly romantic tale of jealousy and revenge. I especially loved its distinctive prose, which is ornate and stripped-down by turns.
—Christi Nogle, author of Bram Stoker Award® winning first novel *Beulah*

"*Merciless Waters* seethes with feminine rage and drips with sapphic desire. Knowles weaves a story full of unreliable queer women doing unthinkable things, laces it with dark magic, and dyes it in revenge. Gripping, immersive, and relentless, you'll find no heroes here."
—Evelyn Freeling, Editor of *Les Petites Morts*

MERCILESS WATERS

by Rae Knowles

BRIGIDS GATE™
PRESS

Merciless Waters

Copyright 2023 © Rae Knowles

This book is a work of fiction. All of the characters, organizations, and events portrayed in this story are either products of the author's imagination or are used fictitiously. Any resemblance to actual events or locales or persons, living or dead, is entirely coincidental.

All rights reserved. No part of this publication may be reproduced in any form or by any means without the express written permission of the publisher, except in the case of brief excerpts in critical reviews or articles.

Edited by Elle Turpitt
Proofread and formatted by Stephanie Ellis
Cover illustration and design by Daniella Batsheva

First Edition: November 2023

ISBN (paperback): 978-1-957537-71-9
ISBN (ebook): 978-1-957537-70-2
Library of Congress Control Number: 2023941369

BRIGIDS GATE PRESS
Bucyrus, Kansas
www.brigidsgatepress.com

Printed in the United States of America

For Kristen.

Content warnings are provided at the end of this book

CHAPTER ONE

When the sun strikes violet hues through the cloud cover, I know the gods are angry with me. I do everything I can think of: swallow three strands of Lily's hair, push all the dust on my headboard into a pile, braid and unbraid frayed rope, then braid it again. None of it works. They still throw purple glimmers into the sunrise like noxious fumes. This is their warning. And I learn how they will punish me the moment I see him floating. His pruney fingers cling to driftwood as he coughs out a sputtering sound.

I am about to lose her again.

Rolling waves are the only sound, the rest of us still asleep below deck. His flapping arms beat the water's surface as his eyes roll.

I see you.

His blistered mouth opens in the shape of a plea, and I feel Lily's love slipping away. A seagull taunts me from a hot breeze overhead, tells me as much. I'd hoped it wouldn't be so soon. I thought I had more time.

I wish he would drown.

But the gods will not be so kind.

Scales brush against my ankle, and I glance down to see Ambrose winding through the bow's wooden railing, his alternating stripes of black and white a gray blur. His little costume makes him look like our prisoner, but he is not. As he slithers from the deck, his body coils in the air, and he breaks the water's surface with barely a splash. I think he might be freer than any of us.

Tahi's voluminous curls lift in the wind as she ascends from the crew's quarters. She is never far behind him.

"He went for breakfast," I say.

She nods. Morning light kisses her golden skin, her black hair stark against the blinding blue sky. My body clenches, as if I can stop her from looking over the side, become a statue for both of us. It doesn't work, of course. Her chin dips toward the lapping waves, and though her thick curls cover her face, in my mind I see her brow arching, warping her tattoos as she spies him bobbing. The timer is set on Lily's love. Tahi will save him, and the countdown begins.

Time jumps for me then.

I am aware of the others waking.

Of splashing.

Heaving sounds of strong women with calloused hands.

When he begins flopping about my freshly mopped wood, I descend to my quarters, clutching the banister as my head swims and dots trail about my vision. His sopping clothes smack the deck, and I press my ear to my shoulder to dim the sound until I can stow myself away in my chambers and shut the thick wooden door behind me.

The bed is a mess of twisted sheets. I run my palm against the linen where Lily slept, feel the curves of her in the mattress. She must be with him already, though I didn't see her, too sick with loss. My face hovers above our shared bed, I breathe in her lavender scent. How many nights do I have left? Grief threatens to take me. I push it back with a thin hope that Ambrose bit him in the sea. That venom courses through his thieving blood, binding his muscles and drawing foam from his blistered lips. The thought steadies me.

I survived it before. I can do it again.

As I rub my bed linen between my fingers, I remember. Many dangers lurk on the ship. Especially for a man. Though the gods may have brought him here, they will not look favorably upon his presence. It's unnatural. He does not belong here. And Ambrose may have bitten him already, or he might tonight or tomorrow.

And the pigs will eat most anything.

And the sea is deep and choppy and cold.

And I have venoms all my own, if it comes to it.

I picture a pile of bones, bleached from sun and salt. My lungs fill and my back arches. Lily will return soon, and I cannot let her see the fear in me. I hop to my feet, pull the sheets tight over the mattress and tuck them in at the sides. I fold our blanket in the way Lily likes, position our pillows just so. My tiny mound of dust still rests on the headboard. I clear it away with a swift finger, unwilling to give Lily any ideas she doesn't already have. Padding steps draw closer to the door.

The door hinges creak as she opens it. They need oil. And I look upon Lily as if for the first time. For the last time. I study every detail of her hair, blanched by sunlight and waved by humidity. Her skin remains pale, as if immune to tanning. As if she carries her own darkness. And she does. Her own little shadow trails her like a loyal companion. Almost as loyal as me. She moves in slow motion as she slides over our threshold. Her lilac eyes dart and flutter, her thin dress dances around her slender frame, overjoyed at the opportunity to graze her body.

"What are you doing down here?"

I rub my dusty hand on my trousers and hope she doesn't notice. "Just straightening up."

She makes a satisfied sound. Already I can sense the gap closing within her. Her dissatisfied air has fortified. I smelled the craving in her blood these past few months. And now she has her prize.

"Surely you saw—"

"The man?" I flush from my tone. "Yes, I saw him."

"Such a lonely thing." She approaches, reaches out her hand. "To be lost at sea." Her fingertips caress my cheek, and she smiles like a threat.

"Miracle he survived." I swallow my displeasure.

"Thank the gods, yes." She kisses my chin, and my heart flutters. It is shameful how she's entwined me in her web. Shameful, inevitable ecstasy.

"What will we …" I say it through shut eyes. I want this moment to last.

"We'll prepare him a room of course." Cold covers me and I know she's pulled away. My open eyes confirm it. She is staring out the porthole window now. "It might be nice, for a change …"

I want to vomit.

"Having a man onboard."

The violet clouds made a promise. The gods never lie.

"Why don't we join the others in the dining hall? Dana is preparing breakfast." She asks so simply, as if a great end for us is not brewing.

"Of course," is all I can think to reply.

The ship tips around us on our way through the hall, jostled by unsettled seas. Lily's love, too, is an unstable thing. Erratic, like the flight path of a starling. She walks lightly on bare feet. Always on bare feet. And there's an eagerness to her steps. I remember when she'd approached me so, in the beginning. My own heartbeat is a ticking clock, but I can't alarm the others. Can't will it into existence any more than the gods already have. I hear murmurs and spurts of laughter, the sound of waves against the hull. Lily slips inside the heavy door, and I'm consumed by unwelcome levity.

The dining hall is a long corridor bookended by the kitchen and door. A table stretches through the center, and light strains its way through porthole windows to illuminate the wood grain and flashing eyes.

The man sits at the head of our table, scorched. His skin an angry shade of vermillion and his hair bleached— but not the ashen white of Lily's locks. Instead, it's a sallow jaundiced color that speaks of pus and disease. I smell the rot coming off him. He is not one of us.

Yinka fawns over him, straightening his collar, pushing errant strands from his eyes. Her flaming red hair is tamed into twin braids close to her skull. Her green eyes tell me about the sadness in her that wants to fix him. It hangs gritty in the air like brine. Behind the butcher's block, Dana chops heads off fish with a meat cleaver. Whacks punctuate the banter between Tahi and Moryana, who lean against our long table and arch their backs and brows.

Dana appears from behind the kitchen counter holding a silver plate piled high with chopped fish. Yinka sees her coming, or smells her, and grasps the plate.

"Shall I fetch some wine for our guest?" Dana asks. She wears brown trousers and a fitted gray jacket, a white tufted shirt beneath. Practical, like her short, blunt hair, which she lobbed off with a filleting knife some time ago.

"No," I say.

"Yes," Lily says. She smiles at me.

Dana shrugs, smirks, heads back to the kitchen to fetch it.

The man stares down at our offering, temptation in his eyes. "Could we, perhaps, throw it on the fire?" He nudges translucent flesh with his fingertip.

The pigs never complain.

"Of course," Lily says. She can be accommodating when she likes. "It's been far too long since we've had any company." Her fingers walk the length of his shoulders. My stomach tips like the hull on the waves.

Someone takes the fish to the deck for cooking, maybe Tahi, maybe Moryana. I can't be sure. It's all blurry.

"How many days …"

"What happened when …"

"How did you ever …"

Lily's and Yinka's questions blend together into a dizzying stream of consciousness.

He slurps wine now. Lily holds a glass in her hand, uses it to hide her mouth like a secret. My heart pounds away our time together.

Every putrid word from his lips is met with wide eyes and fascinated grins from my brood. I can only look on in veiled horror.

Finally, Yinka's heavy heart overtakes the novelty of him. She slumps into her chair, resumes her usual far away pose.

"I could've died out there," the man boasts.

"All natural things die," Yinka mutters to the open space around her. "Only poison is forever."

If he heard her, he doesn't show it.

"I don't think we've caught your name," Lily says.

Don't name him. Don't make him real.

"Reginald."

My heart sinks.

"Reginald, where is it we should escort you?"

"I wouldn't want to be any trouble," he says, though trouble is what he is.

"It's no trouble."

"I was headed along the Faroe Islands when we capsized. Are we far from there now? I would never be such a bother as to take you out of your way."

"We have no way," says Yinka.

Reginald's eyebrow perks.

"What she means to say," Lily adds, "is that we would be happy to bring you to port in Amsterdam."

"Shall you check with your captain?"

We women exchange looks. *What will you tell him, Lily?*

"It's quite alright," Lily says.

Tahi smirks. She's returned with cooked fish. I wonder whether the pigs will notice their missing portion.

His waterlogged fingers poke at the grey flesh. It crumbles and sticks to his skin. His tongue darts in and out of his blistered mouth, ushering morsels stuck in his mustache and beard down into his gullet. How can Lily even consider this?

Yinka wanders away. It is her time of day to stare at the sea in silence. No one questions where she goes.

"We must get you out of those clothes," Lily says, yanking his tattered shoulder.

With both hands, he scoops the remaining musculature into his maw, gnashes it and bobs his head in eager agreement. Her fingers slide down his arm as she steps toward the door, and he follows her like she's a siren crooning her song. Uneven ticks of my pulse dim then fall away.

My time is up.

CHAPTER TWO

Gathering the scraps and bones and eyeballs, I usher our catch to the pig pens. It is dark below deck. So few windows. Squeals of anticipation greet me as I draw close. It's not usually I who feeds them. Yinka insisted on keeping them, after all. Her heart is too soft and too young for the sea. But when I saw her in a particularly heavy state, I knew the waves would keep her many hours. So, needing distraction from my troubles, I took it upon myself to satisfy the pink beasts.

One, two, four …

I count eight. There were nine previous, were there not? Tossing the chum into the pen, the ravenous creatures migrate to the starboard side and reveal their missing comrade. He lies swollen, stiff. I slip between the rails while the live ones chomp. No blood stains the hay. No obvious injury. Old age, perhaps. The dead one's stagnant gaze is fixed on a spot on the roof. I look up to see what he saw. Bowed wood. As good a thing as any, to see in the last. With a nudge of my boot, I declare him dead. I think of notifying the others, but now that there's a man aboard to feed, I think better of it. As I said, pigs will eat most anything, and our nets have been slim as of late.

I must think of anything but Lily. It will do me no good to dwell. I exercised every approach when it happened with Dalia. Begging. Playing coy. Spying. Sneaking. Raging. It was all for naught. She cannot be moved by any feeling. A deep breath steadies me. All I can do is wait. Wait, and perhaps plan.

The pigs are a hefty line: slurping and chomping and cracking thin bones. Their tails swat fungus gnats with circular swings. A faint memory lingers just out of reach from my mind. Some familiarity about the wriggling movement, the tail so much like hair in a whirling sea. I sigh and push it away. It's no use trying to remember *before*. Even if I could latch on, see the pictures of before and recall the names and faces, it would make no difference. Whatever happened then, I resolve myself to the sea. It is my present, my future. There is no past.

The straw stinks of urine and burns my eyes, so I slip back through the slats of the pen and make a mental note to remind Yinka to clean it out. I'll wait until her sad moment has passed. It's only fair.

I wind through the hallway, hear Dalia muttering to herself. Her brown hair is thick and straight. She wears it loose, letting it frame her round face and fall heavy about her almond eyes. In the dark of night, I hear her singing sometimes. Old songs we all come to know. Her voice is crisp and clear, ever on key. It's just another thing to envy her for.

I can't help but be bitter as a black coffee, even though it happened so long ago. Those nights when Lily warmed her bed instead of mine. The memory of their stolen kiss as thunder rolled, that one is clear and sharp as the day it was made. I tell myself I forgive Dalia. But forgiveness runs contrary to our making. In truth, I don't think any of us know how. Luckily, she slips inside her quarters and shuts the door before I have to make pleasantries. It is a great relief. There's little I detest more than pretending.

But the bigger evil meets me on the steps, and I climb to the deck. The man, Reginald, as he calls himself. A puffed-up name for a squirrelly man. I see my brood have gifted him fresh clothes, a crushed teal velvet coat jacket and a white linen shirt, tan pants and scuffed brown leather boots that came with the ship. I wonder whether he feels their first wearer. Whether he can hear whispers from their uneasy spirits. He looks comfortable enough, pausing there on the landing and shooting me that satisfied smile. Why are men ever posing as satisfied? I add it to the list of my reasons to hate him.

"You're not pleased I'm here," he says, like he's made some revelation.

I say nothing.

He examines the banister, it's fine wood and brass trimmings. "How does a group of women such as yourselves come by such a ship?"

It is my turn to wear a satisfied smile. "'Tis an expansive world, full of many horrors and misdeeds. On this, men do not have a monopoly."

He *hmphs*. "Lucky you found me." He knocks on the wooden wall with his fist as if performing some inspection. "It's lunacy, not having even a single man aboard to captain such a vessel."

"We have no need of men."

His lips stretch and tighten like a cow chewing cud.

"So you must think." He steps down toward me, squaring his shoulders with mine, and I think he might plow me over, but he steps aside at the last moment, continuing down the steps.

"Careful of the pigs." It's all I can think to say. He doesn't break stride. My anger ties a knot in my chest. "And of Lily." That makes him pause. He turns his head to face me. "She's a fickle creature. You may hold her interest for now, but she will sour. And when she does …" I climb to the landing. Let him wonder about my words. "As I said, careful of the pigs. They'll eat most anything, you know."

I return to my room, replaying the conversation again and again in my mind. I think of much better things to say, clever retorts, needle-point threats. The sight of Lily folding a pastel yellow dress over the bed halts my internal confrontation.

"What are—"

"Thought I'd spend the night with Reginald."

It's a gut punch, though I expected it. "Reginald."

"Yes, poor thing. Adrift at sea for god knows how long. He must be so in need of the company of a woman."

Her love slips through my fingers like so much cold water. "And you … are in need of the company of a man?"

She holds the corner of her dress taut, pauses, but doesn't look at me. Then resumes folding. "Yes, I suppose it's been something on my mind."

I nod my head as the words take root. Lily places the dress in her satchel, with such love and care you'd think it might be an infant. A stack of folded garments rests beneath it. Already her lavender scent is fading from the air.

"I see."

She crouches to secure the buckles, then stands up to face me. "Don't be cross with me, Jaq. It's just for a time." Her smooth lips graze my cheek like the end of a story. The last grain of sand fallen through the hourglass. With each smack of her bare feet on the wooden floor, I think of another way to kill him.

Step.

Throw him overboard into a churning sea.

Step.

Rub rat pelts on his clothing until Ambrose takes a bite.

Step.

Bludgeon him with a spare metal rod.

Step.

I see all the others, their many-colored eyes bulging and their faces turning blue, the sea foam collecting about their thrashing limbs, the slick sweat dribbling into their eyes, soaking through their clothes, their knees buckling as their hearts give out. There are so many ways.

I need only choose one.

She closes the door behind her, and I slink over to the lowest drawer. It squeals open, another thing needing oil in the tracks. I parse the layers of tissue. Crinkling and white as snow, they cover my secret thing. My favorite thing. The glass is cool on my palms, and I clasp it with the gentleness I would my own beating heart. I close my eyes for a moment. Think of all the rituals that brought it into being. The full set of teeth. Tahi had to help. Of everyone, she remembers most of the old ways. She swore not to tell a soul, swore on the most intimate threads within her. I clutch the bottle to my breast and feel them squabbling. The ship is steady inside. I know this without looking because our ship is steady. The sea is calm and smooth as glass.

Pressed against me, I will it to take the fury from my heart. I need to be as cool and collected as today's sea if I'm to succeed. Lily will not make it easy. She'll hover over him like a fly. I send my anguish into the glass, feel vibrations around my fingers. I think of everything I can: Lily and Dalia together, the click of the buckle on Lily's satchel, the smacking of her feet on bare wood, the coldness on her sheets, the absence of her smell.

I hear it now, the tiny sails clicking against the side of the glass as the miniature ocean swells. My chest lightens. My shoulders relax. I hold my secret thing aloft like a baby bird. The sun from the window illuminates the tiny sails, my ship in a bottle. My tiny sea beats its deck with malevolent waves. If I look closely enough, I can see them. Skittering around like ants. If they scream, I can't hear them. Such minuscule vocal cords now. They are my prisoners, my pets. And I like to keep them close.

The ritual was old and required sacrifice, but well worth it to see them here, now. To have this vessel into which I can pour my grief, my rage. The insect sailors wanted naught in life but to take, and now, in their little bubble, they take what I give them. Within the bottle, dark clouds form. They swirl and thicken, but never escape the bottle's open mouth. My fingernails bend against the unyielding glass, and I realize how hard I'm gripping it. Bolts of electricity crawl about the clouds like flittering fireflies, then join together and strike the foremast. I imagine the men screaming. They scurry below deck like so many fleas to escape my storm. I scratch at the glass.

"Do you feel him?" I whisper. "Wearing your clothes?"

I tap with my nail, a great clinking sound, and imagine them covering their ears.

"Would you like another little friend?"

Ambrose slides beneath the door. No place on the ship is off-limits to his svelte, agile body. He regards me. I rewrap the bottle in its protective tissue and stash it away into the drawer. The sound of paper folding against itself is much like the crisp sound of Ambrose's body against the wooden floor. I welcome my friend with open arms.

Come, brother.

He hears my thought and abides, drawing close with his flicking tongue and lying across my crisscrossed legs. His vertical eyes fix on mine. His head hovers. I extend my palm, and he turns his head, allowing me to stroke his smooth scales. I touch the places where black stripe meets white, count them. There are twelve.

"How was your hunt today?"

He cocks his head, once again tastes the air. *A fine hunt,* he seems to say.

"And what do you think of our visitor?"

Ambrose's eyes narrow.

"You hate him."

He coils around my arm and shows off his strength.

"I knew you would."

His color turns sallow about his nose, a yellow tinge staining his otherwise perfectly black-and-white form.

"Perhaps tomorrow I'll join you in the sea."

Ambrose grips the length of my arm with his muscular body, inches up my shoulder.

15

His smoothness caresses my neck and I feel his tongue flick about my ear.

"Will you watch him for me, Ambrose?"

I'm nervous asking. Tahi is his true master. He owes me nothing.

As quickly as he came, he slides down my other arm and leaves through the crack beneath the door. Though he hasn't answered my request, I remain hopeful. Ambrose is a swift creature. Cunning. There is nowhere on the ship he cannot go, and he would make a most efficient spy.

Exhaustion hits me. Pouring my feelings into the bottled ship has been a relief, but is also draining. I climb into bed, atop the covers. Nestle in. Sleep takes me quickly and without mercy. I slip into a dreamless hole.

CHAPTER THREE

I remain in my room for an indeterminate time. Thoughts of Lily in the interloper's embrace keep me from peace. I dream of bloodstained waters, a child abandoned, clawing his face to ribbons. I wake coated in sweat, nauseous. I sleep and wake and sleep again. Perhaps many times. To leave my room feels an impossibility, so swallowed up by grief I am. But, finally, I dream of a night when Lily was mine. I recall her fawning over my smart dress and unusual style of hair. This inspires me.

So, when I decide to emerge from my quarters, it is in my finest suit, tailored to my body as if by the gods themselves. In my long mirror, I examine the lapels, crisp black. Without Lily's hands to help, it takes several minutes to fasten my fine, gold cufflinks. Those came with the ship. I found them in the captain's quarters and ferreted them away for a special occasion. I can think of no more special an occasion than this: winning back Lily's heart from an evil dragon. Or a man called Reginald. I shine my boots with an oiled cloth, fifty strokes over each toe. I secure my hair into plump braids on the long side, freshen the shave on the other. I smudge black pigment beneath my bottom lashes. This is her favorite way to see me. She will find it hard to ignore.

It must be late in the day when I reach the deck. Ambrose has cozied up in a coil. He absorbs the last warmth of day, still slick with seawater from his afternoon hunt. I greet Dalia, ignore Yinka (her eyes so full of sorrow, I roll mine and avoid her gaze), and shuffle up to Tahi and Moryana.

"It's a fine breeze this morning; we sail quickly."

Tahi smirks but says nothing about my polished appearance. "Good thing, too."

Moryana nods, puts her hand to her face as a shield as she looks out over glittering waves.

"And why's that?" A thrum in my chest and belly.

"Ask her yourself." Tahi eyes behind me, and I glance over my shoulder to see Lily, both arms slung around Reginald's shoulders. My ears heat with blood.

My boots carry me to them without my consent, and the words pour from my lips before I can think them through. "What is the meaning of our full sails? To where do we travel with such haste?"

A coy grin surfaces on Reginald's mouth. His sunburn has healed, leaving a tanned glow across his cheeks, which are far fuller than last I saw him. "We travel to La Serenissima. A long overdue trip."

Lily's eyes hold a secret. I address her directly. "Overdue?"

"Aye." Lily's word is simple, yet stirs something foreign from a dry, dim place.

A thirsty beast wakes inside my gullet. I fight to sustain my posture.

"I'm only just remembering," she says. Reginald laces his fingers through hers, as if he holds her upright. "I think it's important we return."

I swallow the lump forming in my throat. "The port in Amsterdam is far closer. Surely we should take our guest to his destination before we consider alternative routes."

"I've no need to get to Amsterdam. La Serenissima was always my ultimate destination, and when I learnt of Lily's desire to dock at the very same port, well ..."

His insufferable look of satisfaction shrinks me. I am a petulant child. "May I speak with you alone?" My eyes urge Reginald to leave, but he remains by her side. His unfortunate visage occupies the space that should be mine. "Below deck, perhaps?" My cocked eyebrow pushes him away, and he has no choice but to step back.

Lily nods and follows me down the stairs, where the windowless hall extinguishes the daylight. In the near-dark, the wooden walls press in from both sides. Lily leans against one side of the passage which is too slender for me to pass her should I desire it. Though I could not think of a single reason I should want to depart her. The sea rolls beneath us, a cloying reminder that Lily's world has turned on whilst I slept.

"What is the meaning of this? He stands beside you as if you are some prize hog he's won." My voice cracks.

"You've slept for some time, Jaq." She grasps my cufflink and twirls it between her finger and thumb. "Much has changed."

I scoff. "What could've changed other than yourself?"

She stares into the jeweled embellishment. "I think ... I'm beginning to remember something, from *before*."

My head swims. We are not meant to remember. I become dizzy and catch my fall on the same wall Lily leans upon, and my body brushes against hers. She takes a callow step back.

"You are mistaken." I wipe cold sweat from my temple.

"I am not." She catches a drop of perspiration rolling down my neck and sucks it off her finger. I reach for her hand, but she pulls back. It's all the fault of the dragon. *Reginald.* Saliva fills my mouth.

"Have you gathered what's needed for tonight?"

My thoughts circle. *Tonight?*

"The moon rises full. Have you forgotten?"

No. Have I let such time pass?

"Of course you have. Locked away in your room like some domesticated cat." She reaches for my face and my chest swells, but rather than lean for a kiss, she touches the shaved half of my head. She's always liked the feeling. "Well, it's tonight. Best get going."

She ascends the stairs, the daylight blurring her to shadow, and I recede to my quarters. There is much to do, so little time to consider what Lily meant by remembering *before.* She must be mistaken. A dream swirled too vivid and too strong. It lingers in her mind. That is the explanation. The only rational one for such a harebrained belief.

A little light roars to life inside me as I remember Reginald—even the thought of his name lands a sour taste on my tongue—won't be welcome at the ritual. I think of Lily crushing herbs with her mortar and pestle, of slipping them under his tongue, of unconsciousness cracking his head on our fine wood floorboards.

I shake the distraction from my mind. It's time for collection. I usually grant myself a week to prepare for the full moon, and now have mere hours. I go over my checklist:

An offering
A blessing
A plea

I start with the cumbersome one, an offering. That gull has deserved its end since it mocked me. But how to catch him?

I tear my closet apart. It's easier to do so with Lily's things removed. That's a searing pain I'd like to offer, though I'm not willing to part with it.

No time for that now. I chastise myself. Without Lily here, I must point out my own folly.

I toss old shoes, crumbling leather belts, a gossamer shawl behind me. I find it rusted in a corner. A small cage, the perfect size.

Yes, gull.

Now it's to the kitchen, where I wrap bits of fish in a cloth and stash it inside my chest pocket. In the linen closet I find a tablecloth, white. We won't need this for some time. It won't be missed. I find myself on the starboard side of the ship.

There's no ritual for catching seagulls, at least not one that I know of, so I must use my wit. I lie on the deck and cover my body with the tablecloth, placing the bits of fish on my chest before tucking my arms beneath the fabric. Now I wait.

It's blinding white, and stale air smothers my breath to a light puff. I hear a squawking and know it's close, but I must be patient. Sweat beads at my brow and hairline. I feel it roll from my temple to my ear. My clothes grow damp where my body meets the deck. A shadow passes over.

Yes, gull.

A squawk and another shadow circles, then hovers above, creating a small pool of shade.

Patience.

When I feel its webbed feet land on the soft of my belly, I spring to action, wrapping the gull in the tablecloth in a blink. It shrieks, flails its wings, but it's no use.

I am far stronger than you, gull, and I'll have my revenge.

If anyone has seen my little trick, they've left the deck before I can spot them. I twist the tablecloth, so it becomes a gull-sized rucksack, and return to my room victorious. The gull goes easily into my cage, and there it watches me, knows I have bested it.

You'll think twice next time, gull. Though I know it won't have a next time.

The blessing is simple and requires less preparation. I scrawl my words on parchment with ink and quill.

Bless our ship, Scylla. May we sail forever with the favor of the gods.

We must burn the plea. And since eating Lily's hair didn't work, perhaps burning it will. I rip the blanket from our bed and inspect her pillow. Her strands are faint against the white sheets, but I spot two and collect them, stowing them away in a small glass jar I keep for such things.

I am ready. I smooth wild hairs into my greasy mane. Dampness lingers in my underarms, and I know my finery will need a thorough cleaning. I glance down to smooth my jacket and notice a white trail of excrement.

So you'll have one last laugh, gull.

I remove it with care and manage to avoid soiling my hands. Looking over my offerings, I can't help but think they are not my most thought out gatherings, but they were selected with intention and will have to do.

In the golden hours before nightfall, I wash my face clean of pigment. I brush the braids from my hair, remove my boots and oil them, and strip my ornate clothing, hanging it with care. I lace a garland of dried eucalyptus betwixt my pleated mane and watch through my porthole window as the sun admits defeat and surrenders its light to an endless sea.

The air is charged with feminine power. There is magic in the wind tonight. Above, a full moon smiles. Only whispers of cloud obscure the view. I am almost wholly myself, my naked skin goosed beneath the moonlight. Her approval runs through me, and, for the moment, I forget my troubles.

Offerings go in the center of the circle, so I place my cage there. The others ascend from their quarters, some one by one, some in pairs. Freed from their clothes, their unblemished skin is a cool toned palette, shades of beauty from every corner of the Earth. We are ghosts upon the sea, spirits blessing the water. We circle around the main mast and await our Captain.

Her steps are so smooth. It is as if she floats upon the air, or is one with it, with her ebony skin like crushed velvet and her gleaming emerald eyes.

"Lucinda." We say it in unison and take a knee like a dance.

Lucinda lowers her chin, and we rise. She's cloaked in white fur—mink most likely—and her presence, so rare and so precious, gives us strength. She is timeless as the air we breathe, steady as the tide, wise as the North Star. More offerings are placed in the center circle: a fish that still flaps, a mouse that squeaks within a linen bag, live ivy, a bottle of perfume with gold embellishments.

"We gather to honor the moon." Lucinda's voice is a song. It draws our eyes to the fullness of the orb's majesty, and clouds step aside, as if knowing their place.

"We free ourselves of worldly things, for though we were once of this world, we are no longer."

My sisters step in time to her melodic voice, moving in a slow circle around the offerings. I flow with them, and we are of one body. One arm closes around Tahi to my right, the other around Moryana to my left. Each woman laces her arms in turn, and we become a single naked beast of many eyes and appendages. Lucinda sings tones of grief and rage, sacrifice and freedom. Tears flow from our myriad eyes and groans erupt from each woman, one by one, as we release our pain to the care of the heavens. It's a rapturous dance, one we do not take lightly. With a sung note in C minor, Lucinda ends her song. My arms are heavy upon my sisters' shoulders. I feel our collective weight. We are emptied. Our tear-streaked cheeks and our breasts slick with sweat, we collapse in sync.

Lucinda steps into the circle beside our offerings. "You have each brought a gift for our gods. May they satisfy. May they bring us favor." Her eyes pass over each woman. I watch her watch them. When she gets to Lily, she hovers a moment too long.

"Tahi, prepare the ropes."

Tahi nods and disappears into a fog, which I realize has blown in during our dance. It hangs thick in the air. The gull rustles in his cage. The fish does a dying flap. When Tahi returns, she ties the offerings together, and on Lucinda's command, I rise along with the other women and lift the rope, letting the offerings dangle like chimes. We walk to the starboard side, forming a line along the banister.

"Speak your blessings," Lucinda says.

We all do at once, a cacophony of sound, and when the last words have left the last women's lips, we drop one end of the rope overboard. It's swallowed by fog.

"Yinka, step aside." She is on the far left and releases her grip and steps away. "Lily." She does the same, and so on, down the line. Moryana holds the last bit of rope, the only thing separating our offerings from the benevolent sea. The gull squawks as if to speak his final words, and then … "Moryana." She drops the rope, which disappears into milky white and makes a muted splash as it breaks the surface.

"Good," Lucinda says. "And now, our pleas." She glides to a nearby, mounted torch and ignites it, as if by some magic. "I remind you; your pleas are silent. They are your own. Speak them to no one, and perhaps the gods will listen." I retrieve the glass jar from beside the capstan where I stashed it as the other women mill and sieve, fetching items of their own. Wordlessly, I approach Lucinda, her torch flaming like a devil's eye in the night. My hand trembles as I hold Lily's hairs aloft, the warmth of the flame chasing my goosebumps away. The hairs catch before I can drop them, fire snaking up each strand in an instant. The smell of burning singes my nostrils, and Lucinda tilts her chin as if to say, *well done.*

I don't watch what the other women burn. That is their business and their business alone. The ritual finished, we share an exhaustion unknown to most. Yinka slinks down the stairs, and I move to follow her, but not before I hear a mumbled voice through the fog. It's Lucinda's, and she says, "Lily, I'd like to speak with you in my quarters."

CHAPTER FOUR

Ordinarily I fall into a swift sleep after the full moon ritual, but tonight my curiosity overtakes my fatigue. I descend the stairs, but rather than turning into my quarters, I follow the hallway, black as the midnight zone without a torch or candle. Lucinda stays in the captain's quarters, at the stern of the ship. There is a quiet way there. An unseen way. I feel along the wall as I draw close, searching for notches with my fingers. I find my target, a carved handle in the wood, and slip into the storage area adjacent to her quarters. There I wait.

I hear Dana and Moryana, whispering of their offerings before the hall goes quiet. I hear only one door open and close. *Interesting.* Perhaps they are bedding together now. I would not be surprised by this, our beds are warmed frequently, our companions often shifting. Lily and I were the only constants. Well, as constant as Lily can be. The others don't know loyalty as I do. They don't suffer commitment. They are made of less durable fabric than I.

When I hear a single set of footsteps, I assume it must be Tahi. Yinka has already retired. I press my ear to the wall. Strong footfalls raise the hair on the nape of neck. At first, I think Lucinda may be alone, but then I realize Lily is with her, walking in time. This is so like Lily. She does not show fear. She does not *feel* fear. The steps become close then pause. There's a creaking of hinges, a whoosh of air, a shutting. I tense.

"Lilith, do you believe there is anything which occurs on this ship of which I am not aware?" Lucinda's tone is stern. My skin goes pale on Lily's behalf.

"A captain must know the goings on of her ship," Lily replies, her tone cavalier.

When Lucinda speaks again, her voice fluctuates in volume, as if she paces around Lily. "So please explain to me the latest addition to our crew."

Yes, Lily. Please explain.

"He washed up. We brought him aboard. There is not much else to say."

Lucinda *hmms*. "You did not think it prudent to consult me before bedding a man you drew from the sea? Before furnishing him with food and lodging aboard *my* ship?"

"As you have said, a captain knows all the goings on of her ship. I assumed you were aware. That your silence was permissive."

"You made the *assumption*."

"Yes, ma'am."

"I see. You disrespect me, Lilith. You are not an ignorant woman, nor lacking education. Surely there is no version of this world or the next in which you assumed I would approve of such an … interloper."

My heart pounds erratic rhythms in my chest, a furious hope that Lucinda will banish him, toss him overboard for the sharks and the swells and the gulls to pick at.

"Nevertheless, I see your true intention," Lucinda continues. "You wish to indulge yourself with this plaything. Passion and desire are noble pursuits, so I will allow this oddity for a time."

My chest deflates.

"Thank you, Lucinda."

I hear the smile about Lily's lips.

I wait until Lily's steps have dimmed before emerging from my hiding place. I catch sight of her bare buttocks just as she turns toward her door. I stand naked before her, and she waves me closer. I gesture for her to join me in my room, *our room*, I remind myself. Once inside, she drapes herself in my robe, and I'm suddenly aware of my exposed breasts. I grasp the blanket we so recently shared and wrap it about my form.

"You were listening," she says.

I cast my eyes downward.

"Does it please you to know I've evoked Lucinda's ill will?"

"Of course it does not!" My eyes are daggers from the implication, as if I would ever wish Lily harm. "I fear for you."

"Fear for me?" A raised brow. "Is it truly fear you feel?" She walks her fingers across my shoulder, lets them dance upon my neck.

"Why do you toy with me so?" I jerk away, and cold settles in my gut.

"Because I love you."

I am standing.

My palms flail out and the blanket is but a cape upon my back. "So why do you share a bed with this *man*? This sea trash we collected?"

Lily pushes a strand of ashen hair behind her ear. "He amuses me."

I pull the blanket back around my naked form. I know she speaks the truth. For this, I cannot be angry with her.

"You knew I craved the company of a man. You said as much. Many times, in fact."

The memory of each time singes me.

"He sates my craving for the time being. But Jaq, that is not the most *interesting* part. Something is happening." Her features alight with rare enthusiasm. Her lilac eyes flicker. "I *remember*. Not much, but it's something."

"You must be mistaken." I scoff. "It is an impossibility. You know this as well as I. There is only us, here, now, an endless expanse stretching out before us. That is enough. There is no past. We've no need for it." I hear Lucinda in my words.

Lily rises from her seat on the bed. "It's only a few pieces. Fuzzy. But as the days pass with Reginald, they become clearer. New colors begin to take shape."

I decide to humor her. "And what colors have shaped?"

"Lilith Abbot. That was my name." She stands tall, her shoulders square.

"Nonsense." I pace a circle.

"Lilith *Josephine* Abbot." She speaks as if the words themselves are magic.

My jaw hangs aloft. I can do naught but shake my head.

"Give it time. You will see. When we return to La Serenissima, I think I'll really start to understand."

Why would Lily wish to return to where we were found? Where Lucinda took us in? If Lily is remembering … No. It cannot be.

"You speak of unnatural things."

Lily grasps my cheek, her touch featherlight. "Sleep well, Jaq." She slips off my black, silk robe. I swell with desire and have to grip my fingernails into the blanket fabric to keep from reaching out and touching her.

She glides toward the door.

"Lily, wait."

She pauses, a brief hold on sands through the hourglass.

"Perhaps you could stay?"

She looks upon me as she might a child begging for bread. "Another night. Perhaps." And with that she leaves me.

I toss myself upon the bed, crestfallen. The scent of Lily has gone and my head swirls with her strange notions. I close my eyelids tight, let the blackness behind them swirl into every shade of a bruise. My mind wanders from now until then. I reach back inside myself, to before Scylla. It's hard to grasp, like a dream scuttling away upon waking. But bits and pieces come to me when I call, a patchwork of truth stitched together by sense memory.

There was Lily and I and rippling water. Submerged in a frigid sea, we clung to one another, a cold settled deep into our bones. At first, we stared at the horizon. Perhaps distantly, there may have been a shoreline. A far swim, yes, but not impossible to traverse. Despite our long hours adrift, we felt no fatigue, and there seemed no cause for us to remain floating. But an unseen wind kept us from any attempt to reach shore. The water was chains upon our ankles.

I think I recall the curve of her hip, how her skin was warm beneath the waves, and how, as the hours passed, that warmth faded. There was nowhere to go but deeper, so deeper we went. Crashing tides drew us out like a siren song, and as the bottom dropped away beneath us, the Adriatic Sea became like a mother. *Adriana* we began to call her. She wrapped us in sea foam, adorned our hair with algae and kelp. Lily was the first to dive. There was a beat of fear, then the sensation of her grip on my ankle. She pulled me down, and we were both engulfed by her, *Adriana*, the sea so cool and wide. I opened my eyes, only able to see Lily and miles of elusive blue and, to my surprise, the saltwater did not burn.

We swam for some time—-I know not how long, for time itself seemed to buckle and bend like leather. And next I know, for the exact chain of events remains fuzzy, there was a boat. It was a small thing, just an oar dipping below the mirror surface. Movement drew me in, and Lily too. We flocked to it like buzzards upon a kill. There Lucinda found us. She pulled us aboard, embraced us in her lovely arms, skin glistening with beads of moisture.

I try to push my mind to before.

How did we get into the sea?

But I'm pulled from my trance by the sensation of scales over my arm, curling about my shoulder. I crack open my eyes, turn my head to see Ambrose's flicking tongue. He presses his nuzzle to my ear, tongue tickling my lobe.

Jaqueline Dempsey, he whispers. *Jaqueline Fay Dempsey.*

A bolt tears through the fabric of me. *It cannot be.* And yet, so familiar, like a song I've sung many times. Jacqueline Fay Dempsey, yes, that was my name, *is* my name.

"Ambrose, from whom do you learn these secrets?"

He winds off the bed, his plump belly landing on the floor with a splat.

"Ambrose!" But he continues on his path and slips beneath the door. He will not reveal his sources, yet I know who's to blame. It is the dragon, the man who calls himself Reginald. He is the sole variable, the only new thing. He poisons us now with forbidden knowledge, and who may know what pain will result.

But how to dispatch him? Lily will act as a fervent guardian. I must summon Lucinda to my side. Once she comes to understand the ramifications of this intruder, she will have no choice but to side with me, to form a powerful alliance. Lily will not be able to stand against her. She would risk exile. And even Lily would be moved by something so bleak and lonely as isolation. Lily needs her followers, her adorers. She feeds on their fawning like a four-course meal. No, she will not risk exile.

I resolve myself to this purpose, to appeal to Lucinda's love of the old ways. We welcomed something unnatural aboard Scylla, and now more aberrant things unfold. Surely Lucinda will agree to his execution or, at very least, indefinite imprisonment with Scylla's prior owners. She will help me perform the rituals, to collect the many tokens needed to add another pet to my tiny glass farm, then Lily will return to me, unable to abide an empty bed. She will remember that she longs for my kisses upon her forehead, needs me to brush through her locks each evening, delights in my attentiveness. Then all will be as it was, a great wrong righted, with minimal harm in the process.

I climb beneath my white linen sheets and cinch them in close around my form. Swaddled in this way, I feel a measure of comfort. Sleep begins to take me, and as I drift into kind unconsciousness, I think, *I am Jaq of Scylla. Endless present stretches out around me like eternity. I have no past. I need no past.*

CHAPTER FIVE

When I come to the captain's quarters, I find Lucinda scrawling notes in her journal. I rap on the open door.

"Come in," she says without looking up.

I take hesitant steps inside. Everything hinges on this. My recited words, so clear in my head just moments ago, flitter from my recollection. Her quill strokes rough pages, her hand furious as she writes. "Might I speak with you?" I cringe at the sound of my meek voice, but the words are released and cannot be swallowed.

"Are you not already?" She pushes her chair back and grunts, strikes a line through her writing. "Shit, well, you have my full attention now. You've obscured my entire line of thinking." She turns to face me. "So, what is it?"

She has the impatient look of a woman with more pressing issues. But she does not understand, not yet. "It's Lily, well, and me, I suppose."

Her raised brows draw more words from my lips.

"There is something strange happening. Something unnatural. I thought it best to …"

"To?"

"Consult you." I curtsy and bow my head.

"What strange things are happening, Jaq, about which you should have need to inform *me*?"

My cheeks burn. *What if she knows? Knows and cares not?*

"Lily told me, last night, that she—"

"Before or after you spied upon our meeting from my storage closet?"

I swallow a thick lump as Lucinda sighs, rights her chair, and returns to her writing on a fresh sheet of parchment.

"I apologize for my intrusion, I just—"

"Yes, yes I know." She swats her free hand about. "Lily tends to drive you to lunacy. Always has."

I nod, though she is not looking at me.

"Lucinda, I worry for us."

I wait for her to stop writing, for her eyes to widen with concern, but she does not, and they do not, so I continue.

"Lily is saying strange things, convinced of memories from *before*." Surely the look is coming now as Lucinda's heart begins to race in her chest, but it does not. "She told me her name. Her *full* name. She couldn't possibly—"

"I suppose you've not been above deck this morning. Late to rise as usual."

I hear my pulse. "I have not."

"Perhaps you should then." Her hand traces a bold signature, and she rolls the parchment into a tube, slides it inside a glass bottle.

"Is there something … have I—"

"All of Scylla is abuzz with surnames this morning, Jaq." She crosses the room to one of her many porthole windows, where happy light streams in despite the wickedness afoot. I process the words, my brain picking them over and sorting them, and a tentacle winds its way through the circular opening. Its suction cups flare and recede like greedy hands. More tentacles emerge, pale lavender in color, furling and unfurling, reaching. Lucinda places her glass bottle, note inside, in the closest tentacle's grip. It wraps around the object like it is precious to the thing and, one by one, the tentacles slip back through the porthole. Only briefly I catch the gleam of a too-large octopus eye before a light splash tells me the creature has returned to the sea.

"I have reached out to my confidants for guidance," Lucinda says, drawing an expansive breath. "I can only hope they have some experience in these … matters, and may offer their sage wisdom." She straightens her jacket, a fine, burgundy piece tailored to her body with artful precision.

"Is this because of our visitor?"

Her eyebrow cocks. "I should think so."

More confirmation. "All the more reason, I think, that we should dispatch him with great haste. It has been only … how long has it been? No matter. Too long. Too long is the answer and we shan't suffer him another day. Isn't that right? I should be happy to carry out the exec—"

"Jaq, breathe." Lucinda drags sea breeze through her nostrils, gesturing for me to do as she demonstrates. I abide, begrudgingly, but admit the practice does have some soothing effect. "We cannot afford to act rashly. I will wait for the counsel of my betters, and I *trust*," the word comes out with sharp edges, "that you will wait as well."

"Aye." I curtsy, feeling suddenly outclassed by this measured woman of great fortitude.

"You may take your leave."

I slink from her company and imagine myself transformed to some rodent with mange. My plan failed, or at least delayed, I ascend the stairs to the deck. Daylight has burned away the night's fog, and Scylla bucks atop choppy seas. Upon the landing, murmurs greet me as my wandering sisters mill and sieve about the deck with furrowed brows.

"Latu."

"Merrick."

"Kutznetsov."

"Hutton."

"Petroff."

It is a strange chorus of incongruent ramblings, of revelation and confusion and mess. Tahi crouches in a corner, obscured by a barrel. Ambrose is laced around her neck and arms like a living shawl. He faces her and she stares intently into the vertical slits of his eyes, whispering to him. Yinka clutches one of the many ropes tethering our sails, her eyes full of tears and her lip trembling. My feet carry me toward her. Her emotion seems overwhelming, unacceptable, even for sad Yinka.

"What is it, Yinka?"

She repeats the same thing over and over. "Yinka Petroff. Yinka Petroff."

"That's your name, yes?"

Tears free themselves from the confines of her lids, streaming down her cheeks in silence. "Yinka Petroff."

"This is just some illusion." I place my hand on her back, the other over her clenched fists.

She dismisses me with a slow and somber shake of her head. "Yinka Petroff."

"It is only a name, Yinka. What melancholy rears itself within you so?"

Her jaw trembles. "I—I cannot recall."

This is a momentary respite.

"But   " she continues.

A quake in my chest.

"It is as if some *thing* has awoken." She reaches an arm outward, grasps at the air. "I can't quite reach it"—her arm falls —"but nevertheless, it is as if some ghost awoke beside me this morning, bearing the news of my name and with it a profound longing, a loss so deep and wide …" Her breath hitches. Instinctively, I catch her as her knees buckle, but she pushes me aside. I step back, show her my palms.

From my periphery, I spot Reginald, skulking like a latent poison, looking about the deck, no doubt for Lily. And in the moment I am distracted, Yinka sprints. She reaches the banister, clutching it with both hands, then hikes up her peach skirts above the knee, grabs the fabric in one hand and, with the other, launches herself over Scylla's side.

"Overboard!" I scream. I run to the starboard side where Yinka's flash of red hair disappears in time to see a curtain of bubbles erupt from the water's surface. Waves roll and crash, and Scylla tips and sways in the swells. "Overboard!" My throat goes hoarse from the force of it. Dana and Moryana join me at the banister and begin lowering a length of rope. Something takes me then, some dark beast, and I am of a singular mind.

My eyes are daggers when I spot him, frozen, back pressed against the port side railing. My steps could bring down nations as I am made of flaming rage. Before I know it, my hands are wrapped around his slim neck. I hear screaming. "This is your fault!" And it's only by the burn in my throat that I know the sound comes from me. Time goes to sludge. His pulse throbs at his temple. I am fire. I am vengeance. He turns a shade of purple. I think of the lavender octopus and wonder a moment whether I can turn him a similar shade. There's pressure on my chest, and I break eye contact to realize he is pushing me away, and is grabbing at my wrists, trying to pry away my grip.

"I will watch you die." I don't know if I say it or think it loud enough for him to hear, but a bit of snot leaks from his flared nostrils, and fear turns his eyes white.

There's a ringing inside my skull. Day is swallowed by unforgiving blackness. I go cold.

I don't know how long I was gone, but when I wake, I wear a thick coat of cold sweat, iron chains wrap my feet, and the brig's bars come into focus, fuzzy at first, then clear as a spring day. I cough, the air sandpaper on my tortured throat, and hear a faint moaning at my side. I turn to see maroon hair, wet and mottled and strung in clumps over a youthful, freckled face.

Yinka's peach dress is stained dark by the sea and puddles form around her as moisture trails from her garments. Arms wrapped about her knees; she muffles sobs in the folds of her sopping dress. Words break through her hitched breaths and erratic whines, jumbled, but sounding something like "Yinka Petroff."

I push myself to a sitting position and wipe the sweat from my forehead. Footsteps echo from down the long hall.

"Hello?" The word is another painful reminder of my screaming.

"You're awake." I know the voice before I see her; Tahi, and when she comes into my limited view, I see that Ambrose has taken to sleeping atop her dress hem about her breasts. Her usually warm toned skin looks sallow in the faded light of the brig. Shadows accentuate her tattoos, and her expression holds swaths of confusion and a measure of satisfaction.

"You've caused our friend Reginald quite a stir." A smirk curls her lip.

"And why am I—"

"Lucinda asked me to see to it you had shed yourself of all murderous intent before allowing you freedom."

I search her face.

I search myself.

I move to stand, but the chains jerk me backward. "Aye. I was swept away by the moment. I feared for Yinka and it drove me to … well, I will not attempt to murder the man again. At least, without Lucinda's go ahead."

She nods and fidgets with the folds of her skirt. There's a rattling of keys; she unlocks the cell door and swings it wide open on its hinges. I wait for her to uncuff my ankle, then stand and do my best to smooth out my clothing. She moves for the door.

"Aren't you forgetting …"

"Yinka must stay."

"Excuse me, why? Yinka is blameless. It was my temper which was out of line. Surely Yinka will not be punished on my behalf?"

Tahi stares coldly at Yinka and brushes her voluminous hair to one side. "Our sister Yinka was rescued, but only barely and through great struggle. She refused to grab the rope we cast down to her. Dana had to hurl herself into the sea, at great risk, and wrestle our Yinka into submission before we could pull them both back onboard."

I look to Yinka, waiting for her explanation of her resistance at rescue, but she casts her green eyes downward and provides none.

"So it would seem Yinka is determined to surrender herself to the sea, and this we cannot allow."

Tahi moves out of the cell and motions for me to follow her. I feel as if strong forces pull me in both directions, so I stand still in my spot.

"Would you care to remain here with her?"

Yinka slumps her head into her arms and sobs rock her body. I think of Lily and the danger we are all in. "No."

"Then come."

I follow, but leave a sliver of my heart in the cell with Yinka and hope it will be some comfort.

CHAPTER SIX

We change course at Lucinda's bidding, sailing away from the Adriatic Sea and toward open ocean, or so we are told. Strong gusts puff our sails and chase away cloud cover. Warm sunlight dapples our backs through the rigging, and all forces and gods seem to conspire to aid us in reaching our new destination.

"It's not right," Lily complains, her face sour.

Reginald flits about her like a reassuring fly. "Your captain said we would return to La Serenissima after this brief detour. Do not despair, my love!"

I tell myself to ignore this ludicrous proclamation. He knows not what he says, and Lily knows better than to give his fanciful words any weight.

Most of my sisters have settled, rationalizing and justifying their names in this way or that, with the exception of Yinka, who remains in the brig, muttering and chanting to herself in the dark. I hadn't told her another pig had passed. Stiffened to stone it was, when I came to gather one for a visit. Happily, her favorite beast remained plump and lively, and I brought her this visitor.

She'd raised her eyes, and I think I detected the smallest smile before she returned her face to the corner of her cell. It pains me so that she will not commit to sanity. Though I suppose she is blameless in this.

Reginald has discovered a wardrobe of fine clothing. Little does he know he wears only the items my sisters and I have discarded, thought too tawdry or bold or ill-fitting. He prances about the deck in a tan waistcoat and black boots, chest first like a mating bird. I wonder how Lily keeps from laughing at the sight of him. She's remained with him many nights now, and I hope her affections are nearly spent. If not, I harbor a second hope, that Lucinda will receive word from her advisors and allow me to dispatch of him in a way most horrible and suitable to his nature.

"And why is this the first we hear of Lucinda's advisors?" Lily's displeasure is painted upon her scrunched forehead.

"'Tis not our business," Moryana says, tightening a bit of rigging around the mast. "You are too bold, questioning our captain, when you know so little of the old ways, and take such reckless measures with the lives of your sisters, no less yourself." Her wide-brimmed cap casts her face in shadow, layers of darkness upon her face and neck.

"I don't recall asking for your thoughts, Moryana. Please busy yourself, I see a tear in one of our sails, just there." Lily gestures at the smallest fissure in the rippling fabric above. "That is your purview, is it not?"

"You degrade yourself," I say, a low whisper, but Lily hears me. She comes toward me against the wind, which wraps her skirts around her form.

"Envy is a sin," Lily hisses.

I meet her eyes with mine, our mouths close enough to share a kiss. "And why shall I pay mind to Christian sins? You forget yourself, *sister*. We serve the oldest gods. Or do you not remember your making?"

This pushes her from me, and Reginald looks on. I catch the wrinkle in his brow before he can hide his worry. "Old gods?" He looks to Lily. "What is this blasphemy?"

"Blasphemy!" The word comes forth before I can restrain it. "He curses us all then speaks of blasphemy?"

Moryana shakes her head in disapproval before ascending the foremast to attend to the tattered sail. Lily flashes me her warning eyes. She is nervous, a rare emotion from a callous bird such as she. If I frighten him too much, she may lose her bedfellow.

"There is something strange about this ship." He takes Lily by the hand. "I worry for your soul." His too fat fingers smooth away a bit of ashen hair from her cheek, and I imagine her suffering as he breathes into her lovely face. "It is of the utmost importance we get to port in La Serenissima. I fear your fate may depend upon it, both in this life and the next."

She allows his kiss upon her and all else falls away from existence. He touches her fine skin within a dark tunnel, and I forget the shining sun and pleasant caress of the wind. There's a buzzing about my ears. It grows louder each time his lips return to hers, and when he presses his body against her, it is impossible to ignore. I look up the foremast to see its source: a honeycomb pattern, teeming with milky larvae and swarming with adult wasps.

We call them to us, these vicious things. Wasps, snakes, birds of prey. They feel the venom within us and understand Scylla is a home for such things. As I watch the insects hover, feel Reginald's hands upon Lily as if they invade my own body, a single stinging warrior flits down from its nest. It lands upon my shoulder. It whispers a generous offer.

We will kill him for you. Deliver him to us.

I nuzzle my cheek against its armored body, careful not to harm him. I thank him in my mind, and he returns to his brood. A new plan has been gifted to me. Surely Lucinda could not blame me for an unfortunate accident. But how to get Reginald to climb the foremast? He is quite useless at sailing, offers no skills, and seems solely motivated by bedding my one true love. Perhaps there's something to do with that. Yes, the ego of men is quite fragile, and many have fallen while attempting to bolster it, whether to win the favor of a woman or of their fellow brethren. As suddenly as it began, the buzzing stops, and I'm snapped back to the present moment as Lily's lips leave Reginald's, a strand of spittle linking them for a breath before breaking.

"I think I spy a twist in the ropes," I say, shielding my eyes from the sunlight in dramatic fashion.

Lily glances upward. "Where?"

"Just there." I point for emphasis.

Reginald steps closer to the mast. "I see nothing."

"Perhaps my eyes are sharper." My words most certainly are. "No matter, I'll just—" I set a foot upon a barrel and motion to launch myself for the climb, but Reginald steps forth.

"Please, lady." He extends his hand to help me down. "Risk not your health."

I step down, point out the notches in the wood, the places to brace one's foot for the climb. He scarcely listens.

This, too, I predicted. I make a point of swallowing to contain my pleasure.

Lily folds her arms as he begins his assent. I position myself beside her, not accidentally, and use my hand to shield her ever-changing eyes from the harsh daylight.

One foot, then another. With grunting and sweat, he clears two meters overhead, then four. The buzzing begins again. I check Lily's expression to see if she hears, but if she does, she makes no sign of it. I tell my stinging friends he is coming, say it forcefully in my mind so they might hear. A gust ripples the sails, jostling Reginald on his perch, and I delight as his boot slides off a foothold, sorrow as he regains his balance.

"Almost there!" I call.

"I don't see it," he bellows down.

"Just a bit further," I whisper in Lily's ear, "I hope his attempts to pleasure you are more skillful than his eyesight."

She scowls.

Alas, he has reached it. I watch with bated breath as he reaches for the bulge of metal, the only natural resting point for his left hand, where the hive hums with rage just on the other side.

"There!" I say it too loud on purpose. My words startle him, and he clutches the handhold with great force.

In an instant, my friends swarm. First five, then ten, then fifty or more. They attack his arm first, whittling away at his grip with well-placed stings. He yelps like a cornered dog.

"Fuc—wasps!"

Lily's eyes go wide. I dart between her expression and his flailing limbs. The swarm targets his head and neck, and he releases his grip to swat at them, a fool's error. He cries and cries and cries, like a newborn baby but more pitiful, until finally the tumble. A splat of flesh on hardwood.

Before Lily goes to him, she looks to me. I think for a moment she might speak a harsh word, but she only rubs her hand on the shaven side of my head. She's always liked that. Her coy smile suggests something like, *I knew you loved me.* And I think I detect a wink before she takes her place as adoring paramour, kneeling beside Reginald and pulling his shirt this way and that to observe the wounds.

The overture from Lily makes me forget my mission, but it comes rushing back as his groans fill our otherwise pristine deck.

He will survive. Disappointing.

A slightly different angle, a bit of a higher fall, and perhaps I would've been done with the Reginald ordeal. Yet, he groans on. Already his neck has swollen to the width of his jaw, pocked with angry needle point redness at the center of each wound. His arm has expanded such that he appears to lack any wrist, skin stretched so it emits a sheen. Yellow and red, orange and purple. He's a tapestry of color now. I think I have done him a service, far more interesting this way at least. His breath is a quiet rattle, gurgling when saliva blocks the path to his lungs.

I take my leave of the mess, but not before thanking my wasp friends. *You tried your best*, I tell them. Tahi has joined Lily at Reginald's side, and together they drag him to the stairs. I beat them there, lacking desire to be part of the rescue mission, and retire below deck with the hope that perhaps Ambrose is close behind, that he will deliver the last bit of poison to rid us of this nuisance, this abnormality, this thorn.

When I reach the hall, I think better of an afternoon nap, and turn instead to the brig. Yinka has been too strong on my mind as of late, or, perhaps, not strongly enough. I wind through the corridors, dimly lit even in the full light of afternoon, and I hear her quiet sobbing before I cross the threshold.

"Yinka?"

She mutters something in her mother tongue. "Мой брат, мой брат.[1]"

"Yinka, please, speak to me. What ails you so?"

Her under-eyes are swollen and pink as an uncooked salmon belly. Grit from unwashed makeup stains her face in uneven blotches, and her dress is torn at the shoulder.

"Умер мой брат[2]."

I crouch by the bars, grasp one in each hand. "I'd like to help."

Movement at the corner of my eye draws my attention to the hall from which I came, and black-and-white stripes slither toward me. *Have you delivered the death blow to dear Reginald?* I wish to ask, but it is neither the time nor place.

Yinka goes on in her Russian tongue and Ambrose nestles beside me. His tongue flicks in and out, and though his mouth never opens, he is kind enough to translate Yinka's tale.

---

[1] My brother, my brother

[2] My brother, he died

CHAPTER SEVEN

Yinka's Tale:

As translated by Ambrose, the sea krait, with an added bit of flair for his amusement

My brother was a mirror. We shared red curls, a penchant for adventure and tricks, and our parents, of course. In our high and lonely village, they called us "the twins," not only because of the circumstances of our birth but because we could scarcely be found separate from one another. It seemed, at times, I could hear his thoughts and he mine, though this was likely the result of spending so little time apart.

One afternoon, midwinter, we set off with our sled, determined to take the highest hill past the stream. Bolshoi Kunalei in January is as icy as anywhere, and as we traversed the frozen lake our steps were heavy and sure. The prior year, the water had frozen so thick carriages could cross with little concern for cracking it. We had no reason to believe this winter would be any different.

But when the lake began to moan beneath our boots, we knew we had been wrong. We exchanged a look, that's all we needed. No words crossed our lips. We ran. Steps in time and strides equal in length, we crossed the frozen lake as the ice cracked beneath our feet, the crevasse spiraling out like lightning from the weak spot in the center. It was surprisingly loud, I recall. And the cracking sound echoed off the mountain faces, bounced back at us from every direction. I felt my pulse race as the shoreline came into view. We were almost there.

We'd almost made it when the ground beneath opened and swallowed Dimitri whole. Fractured ice beneath my feet, I froze. The water was black, no sign of life, as if he'd descended into the bowels of some other realm. But then I saw air bubbles. Large at first, then a slow and steady stream.

I screamed for him, and my breath hung in the air as mist. Without thought, I plunged my gloved hands into the water below. Cold burrowed into my skin like a thousand bees but still I clutched and waved beneath the water's surface. Finally, I found purchase, the fabric of his coat, and pulled with all my force. But my feet slid on the slick ice sheet, and I found no leverage to pull. Soaked to my elbows, I screamed his name until my throat was hoarse. When finally he surfaced, his lips were blue. His eyes, white and vacant, sat open without purpose.

I shook him. Called his name again and again. I raged at him. Begged him. Tugged and pulled but could not bring him onto the ice. The warmth of his flesh was fading with my strength, and finally I stopped pulling, arm dislocated at the socket, my hands numb. I sat at the hole in the ice, fingers clenched around his jacket while he floated there. The current turned him face down, and I waited for Papa. Surely, he would fix this. Surely, he would know how.

The sun sank beneath distant mountain tops. The wind picked up. My shivering stopped just as the last of the orange glow waned into faint blue. The first of the stars peaked from behind a midnight blanket of sky. I was warm again.

It was then I had strange thoughts.

Dimitri had gone for a swim. *Just a swim*, I thought. *Odd clothes for a swim, but then Dimitri has always been odd. And he must be lonely now. Yes, it's only right I join him.*

I began to sweat. How unusual to sweat, surrounded by ice. I knew it then, and yet I was compelled to remove my coat, my jacket, my gloves, and boots. My socks, soaked through, were last to go. In my undergarments, I faintly remembered I'd been waiting for Papa. But the water seemed to call to me. And Dimitri must be so alone, must want my company, I thought. We were scarcely apart, as I'd told you. It was clear to me what I should do. I dangled my legs in the opening of the ice. Frigid water was a welcome relief for my burning body. I clasped the edge as I might a summertime pool, still clutching Dimitri by the coat, then launched myself down, happy to be near him once again. The current carried us beneath the ice shelf.

How wonderful, I thought. Not unlike the sled ride we'd planned. Wrapping my arms and legs around his stiffening body, I nestled my head in the crook of his neck. It felt natural to return to him this way, like a homecoming to our time in the womb.

"Goodnight, Dimitri."

The words flowed out, accompanied by a parade of air bubbles, my final gift to him. I slept beneath the frozen lake, beside my brother, my twin. Never could we be parted, or so I believed.

But I see now that we've been severed. Permanently severed. Vague sadness always dwelled within my heart, but now it has a name. And the name is Dimitri. It is too much to bear. I wish to join him, wherever he is. So let me free if you've a shred of kindness within you. Free me so I might find my brother, and rest with him a while longer. I have no other wish but this.

Yinka holds the bars such that they frame her face. In her eyes I see the black, rolling lake, the pain so deep and dark it swallows her whole, like an opening in an ice shelf. I know if I free her, she will jump into the sea, but she would not find Dimitri there.

"How can you know this, Yinka? Perhaps this is only a dream. A nightmare so vivid it has you confus—"

"It is no dream!" She speaks to me in English, teeth bared. "It is *before*. I know it as well as I know our own ship. Better even, for while Scylla holds many secrets, the memory of Dimitri is clear and natural as a spring day."

Could it be true? Have we a past after all?

"Lucinda would not have robbed us of such—"

"Don't defend her! How could you? She scooped us up like so many stray cats. Stranded us on this ship to drift aimlessly through choppy seas. Our dubious captain stripped us of all that made us ourselves." Her eyes are once again water as rage softens to despair. "Please, Jaq. There is kindness within you. I have seen it. Let me free. Allow me the dignity to search for my brother, wherever I might find him. In this world or the next."

My jaw hangs aloft. Words escape me. There is too much to consider. The idea that Lucinda has not rescued but bewitched us is … there's a roiling at my center.

"I must think." I step away from the cell, and Yinka withdraws further into it, her gaze dropping to the gritty floor.

She mutters something in Russian. "Время помнил всегда. Оно придет за тобой. Вы поймете тогда.[3]"

Ambrose's vertical eyes narrow with fatigue, and he doesn't translate. So, with heaviness in my heart, I take my leave. Ambrose slithers into a rat hole, to rejoin Tahi I suppose. This *before*, this remembering, has caused a great harm. How long before others sink into melancholy as Yinka has? Or has Yinka simply descended into a madness from which she cannot wake? For the first time in … some time, my mind churns with possibilities. Should we all suffer the same fate? I should think not. And can we truly die? What would Yinka find at the bottom of the sea but coldness and dark and shifting sands?

I must consult Lucinda. There's but one explanation, and it's all to do with Reginald. He is the variable, the catalyst for our current chaos. Lucinda will not abide this, surely. It is one thing to indulge Lily's fancies, quite another to endanger us all.

I set course for the captain's quarters, but I've scarcely left the brig when memory comes for me, too, and some of my questions, at least, are answered.

---

[3] Time remembers always. It will come for you. You will understand then.

Chapter Eight

It would seem that time works in a backward motion. Time or memory. Whether there is any distinction between the two, I know not. But these are the pictures that came forth from a sleeping place in my mind, something distant, but not too much so. Not from *before,* but just after. The story of our making. More accurately, the moments just following it. It comes to me strongly and all at once, and I now understand why Yinka proclaimed such surety in her tale. Accompanying it is a feeling of steadfastness, that of sturdy land. No sense of faint dream memory, as it appeared to me previously, slipping away just as I try to recall the details, but of firm, immovable history.

Jaq, Just After

I awake submerged beneath the icy waters of the Adriatic Sea. Shifting sugar sands caress the back of my thighs, and gentle waves wrap my flowing hair around my face and neck. I should be panicked. There's a vague sense of knowing this, and yet a penetrating calm has burrowed into my marrow. I glance left, unconcerned by the stillness in my lungs, and find Lily. Her eyes crack open, lilac jewels amongst the expansive cerulean sea. She greets me with a smile. I reach for her, and she grasps my hand in hers. Sun glitters off the mirror surface, meters above our heads. Lily has never been more beautiful than this moment. She tugs at my arm, and for a moment, I think she will drag me toward the glistening light. Instead, she helps me to my feet, toes curling into the velveteen sands. As she begins to walk, rolling tides pull our hair upward like ribbons of kelp, and the light begins to fade. We move deeper. Cerulean turns to shades of navy, and I've never felt more at home, more wrapped in deep, unending love. I think of a child in his mother's embrace, and imagine he feels much the same. The Adriatic is our mother, I realize, and Lily shoots me a knowing glance.

"Adriana," she says. The word comes from her lips with a light stream of bubbles. I blow a few from my lungs 'til they're emptied, and I know there's no air inside us any longer. We've no need for it now.

We travel through the deep, cross a sandbar and a reef and, in the blue distance, I spot a towering gray shape. It's larger than either of us, meticulously formed. As we draw near, I see it's a statue carved into stone. Lily pushes off the sandy bottom and hovers some feet above. She runs a finger over the carved lips, smooths the stony brow. There are others spotting the floor. I count five. Women and men etched in stone and left to decay beneath the depths, not unlike ourselves. I examine the faces. The first, a man, older, the age of my father when he passed (yes, I remember this now), with a concerned look, the burdens of his family's welfare upon him. This is how a man sees himself, I think.

The second is a woman, young, with a reckless, wild look about her eyes. I pity her. Stuck in stone, her wildness kept at bay by the sculptor's cruel hand.

The third looks oldest. Pieces have chipped away, leaving it one-eyed, like Cyclops from the old story. From the breadth of the shoulders, I think it's another man. A small flame of anger churns, but before I can interrogate myself on its origin, the cool water smothers it.

The next is further decayed, no face at all, an entire arm missing. I think of some sculptor, etching away at blocks of stone, carving lifelike forms only to drop them into the sea. *For whose eyes are they meant?* I wonder. Some token, perhaps, some offering to a forgotten sea god. I look to Lily who looks to me. Could it be they were meant for us?

We mingle amongst our stony friends, rub the algae that has grown like fur where sunlight penetrates the deep. I feel Lily's fingers wrap around my hips from behind, and turn, slow with the water's resistance, to face her. We dangle in the midst of the waters, no sand or stone or reef to grasp. Grounded only by her firm hold on my hips, I lean closer, touch my lips to hers. She returns my affection with a deep kiss, her tongue drawing mine into her mouth. Naught around us to witness but our stony friends, these silent voyeurs. Passion stirs in my belly like a woken beast. What might our stone fellows gossip about us …

My mind is an empty place. I grasp for names of those I've known but come up empty. Lily's tongue dances over my lips. Her teeth graze my jawline. I realize my nails are sinking into the flesh of her back, pulling a gentle moan from her delicate throat. Her dress, translucent, floats around her like a ghost, and I push the sleeves from her shoulders. The waves are my coconspirators, they draw the fabric down, exposing her supple breasts. The sea pulls me toward them, and my feral need grows. My teeth tickle her nipples. Pressure on the back of my skull tells me to bite, and I oblige, rolling them in turn between my teeth like fine hors d'oeuvres.

Under the immutable eyes of our stone friends, I reach between Lily's thighs, let their cold dead faces watch as I coax her toward her pleasure. She is all desire, all want, as she bucks against my rocking hand. The ocean is a kind partner, lifting and tilting her with the slightest movement of her arms. As she approaches the precipice, I sink my teeth into the sinew of her neck, and her moans refract off the statue garden. My grip on her tightens, as does my bite into her flesh. Her spasming body jerks between my teeth.

There's an odd taste mixed with the salinity, metallic. Soft tissue flakes into my throat, and I release her. Guts clenching, I attempt to read upon her face the length of the damage I've done. Eyes closed, she smiles, enraptured. My shoulders relax, but only for a moment, because a milky trail of Lily's torn matter clouds the water, a ragged hole in her neck where my teeth bore down. I grab her wrist, an impulse, and drag her toward the surface. My heartbeat thrums in my chest, pounds in my ears, and I think for a moment how odd, that it should continue to pulse despite our … circumstance. When we breach the surface, there's confusion in her eyes.

"Your—your neck!"

She shakes her head, and I move her amber hair aside. Nothing but smooth skin.

She reaches for it, checks her flesh with the tips of her fingers. "What's wrong with my neck?"

I flip her hair to the opposite side and search there. "There was a hole—my teeth, I …" There's nothing. Not a mark upon her lovely skin. "Perhaps I imagined it."

She pulls me close, plants a sweet kiss upon my forehead. I wrap my arms around her neck, then recoil when my forearm brushes something ragged. Beneath the surface lies the truth. Her skin is tattered where my mouth had been. Ribbons of flesh cling to her form, dangling in the current.

"Lily, please." I guide her hand to the spot beneath the water. Her eyes grow wide, and her flesh goes pale.

"I don't—I don't understand." Her bottom lip trembles as she feels her ravaged flesh. She rises from the sea, treading water so her neck clears the surface, and once more she reveals her flesh, unmarred.

"It's the strangest thing." I am hypnotized. I run my fingers over the perfect skin where her neck meets her shoulder, then apply the slightest pressure so she sinks inches beneath the surface, where that same skin hangs, mangled.

"It's only below the waves. You're just perfect above."

We go on this way, testing our theory again and again, and always with the same result. A goddess above and a monster below. I don't know how far time stretches before the waves begin to churn. Thunder rolls in the distance, and we share our worries of how to pass the night in the storm. We can't return to land, now too far to see. Not even a distant tree in our sights, just infinite ocean and sky. But as despair sets in, and we start to resign ourselves to being tossed about in the oncoming tempest, a ship breaks the horizon line. Scylla, as we come to learn. And we set our eyes upon our new home, our new sisters, our captain.

So, we gain many things: a home, sisters, a captain, a mother in the expansive sea. Though the ship bucks and dips, it brings no nausea. And when we pass a distant shore, the sight seems repugnant. I think nothing of *before*. And for this, Lucinda, our captain, is glad. She tells us what we need to hear.

"There is only us: our present and endless future. Those who look backward are trapped in folly and regret and will suffer death and much despair. Scylla is without time, beyond it. As are you and your sisters. We have no past. We need no past."

What happens after comes as no surprise. That much is as clear as it ever has been. I find Scylla's former crew locked in the brig, or what is left of them. Scrawny sailors bemoaning their hunger—a feeling I know too well. For I also hunger, and from Lily's ravenous look, I know she shares my craving. They fill my ears with their silly pleas, speaking of pork and citrus fruit.

"Just a sliver of orange," one cries, his face the color of jaundice.

"There's meat in the ice chest. It may have turned but no matter! If you could offer just a sliver—" another whines.

They make me think of butterflies. Twisted pieces of art flittering about. So fragile, innocent in their naivety. Lily plunges her arm through the bars and snatches one by his collar. She lifts him clear off the ground and I see by her face that she's impressed by her own strength. The other men fall back, speaking in whispers out of earshot.

Lucinda looks on from the end of the hall. I turn to her, and she gives permission with a benevolent nod.

The man kicks and whimpers, reaching for his comrades but finding none to cling to. Lily shifts her grip to his slender neck. My hunger flames, and before I understand my own movements, I find myself at her side, tearing at his flesh with fingernails that slice like knives. Hot blood splashes through the bars, anointing my face and hair. So delicious on my tongue, gamey and sweet. I enter a sort of trance. Lily and I are as one, rending his musculature from the bone. His tendons snap happily, and the screams of his crewmates are muted against the glory of fulfilled purpose. The flesh is tender between my teeth. Aye, he is a fine meal!

When we are sated, the world returns to order. Lily and I regain ourselves, and we find our tender friend has become a pile of white bones, clean and dry as if stripped of impurity by a thousand years. His comrades quake from the cell's corner, and I am so full of desire and ecstasy, I pull Lily toward me, caress her slick face with kisses. His iron mixes with her sweetness on my tongue. My hands search her body as they did in the sea, and she grips my hair at the base of my skull with sticky fingers. I prepare to lay her down before the eyes of the shrieking men, but Lucinda's voice echoes from down the hall.

"That's enough."

The spell broken, Lily releases me and I her. We gaze upon one another, never more lovely than this moment, our faces stained red, our teeth filmy with blood.

"You must show some restraint," Lucinda adds. Her weighty footsteps ring clear as she moves toward us, and she glances at the pile of bones. "Collect those and meet me in my captain's quarters. Waste not want not."

We pull each bone through the bars—over two hundred by my count!—and gather them up in our skirts.

Backs pressed against the cell wall, the others watch us with horror on their faces. When we reach the captain's quarters, Lucinda teaches us to carve the bones to points. We make arrowheads, spears, and fine combs for our hair. I've never felt so full, so nourished. A deep craving finally satisfied. I see so clearly now the cause. A simple truth known long to men and only now discovered by womenfolk. We crave violence. So we swallow violent men.

CHAPTER NINE

I race to Lucinda as quickly as my feet will carry me, paying no mind to befuddled looks from Dana and Tahi as I go. I burst through her door, self-conscious of my urgency when she meets me with a questioning glare.

"Captain, I must have your audience immediately."

She sighs and spirals the paper she was reading into a scroll. "What can I do for you, Jaq? I see your prophesying has not ceased since last we spoke."

My cheeks flush. "You must speak with Yinka. Our danger is more present than even I imagined."

She scoffs. "You suggest I take counsel with poor young Yinka, who's descended to madness?"

If her eyes were daggers, I'd be stabbed.

"She—she *remembers. Before.*"

"I assume you mean the names everyone's been murmuring on about, but I can assure you—"

"No. And apologies, ma'am, if I am too bold. But she remembers … another life. In great and vivid detail."

Lucinda rises from her seat.

"She's told you as much?"

I shift my weight from foot to foot. "Well, in a manner of speaking, yes."

"A manner of speaking?"

"She's resorted to her mother tongue, so, yes, she spoke the words and Ambrose was kind enough to translate."

"Ambrose!" Another scoff. "You would take the word of a snake?"

"It's not just Yinka," I plead. "I seem to *remember* too. Just before you rescued us." My eyes search the cresting waves through her porthole window. "When Lily and I … in the sea."

Lucinda takes me by the shoulders. "Jaq, it is not so unusual that you might recall glimmers of the time just before Scylla. But I see the worry in your face. You are my charge, as are your sisters. If danger creeps within our haven, I shall find it and snuff it out."

My tongue searches for the shape of the right words but finds only a saline breeze.

"Now, get yourself to the deck and make haste, woman. We've nearly arrived, and we'll need every sister to bring Scylla safely to anchor."

Something inside screams at me to stay, to convince her to act quickly, but I lack the fortitude to do so. I shrink, nod my head. She hangs back while I corner the hallway and take the stairs to the deck. Green breaks the horizon. I squint and see the impossible—leaves. Leaves and branches of a cluster of trees amidst the endless sea.

I follow their hefty boughs to their bases to find they root in the remnants of a half-sunken ship.

"Hit a reef." There's a hand on my shoulder, and I turn to see Tahi. "Must've been a reef, anyway." Her eyes pass over the same otherworldly sight as my own. "What else could explain it?"

I shake my head, half hypnotized by the sight of it. "It's so strange."

Tahi steps away. "Will you be lifting the sails then?"

"Aye." It's a whisper.

Lucinda's booming voice breaks the stillness in the air. "Bring her safely to anchor alongside. I must consult with my advisor. Certainly, much has been amiss as of late, and it's my duty to ensure Scylla remains a refuge for us all."

Lily and Reginald look on from a distance. She pats his chest as his mouth makes the shape of *impossible*.

"Well?" Lucinda snaps at them.

Lily waves Reginald below deck and joins Tahi in dropping anchor.

An eastern gust pulls us toward the island ship at great speed, and faintly defined figures appear on the deck—what remains of it above sea level.

Scylla drifts toward the island ship at the perfect angle, orchestrated expertly by Dalia at the helm. Sails dropped, we brace on what we can to keep ourselves upright as Scylla slows to a grinding halt.

Lucinda reappears on deck in her finest clothes: a leather vest atop a billowing white shirt, adorned with crests. Ribbons are laced through her braided hair and her black boots' shine rivals the intensity of the sun itself. We extend our ladders so they reach the island ship's banister, and women with solemn faces and uniformed clothes secure them in place. Each wears a brown frock, and though their faces appear not aged past twenty years, their expressions are stripped of all feeling but duty. Their lips are hard lines. Their eyes hold much suspicion.

Lucinda steps upon the first wrung, appearing to feel none of my worry that she may fall into the sea between the vessels. She steps lightly along the ladder, as if the churning waves below merely cheer her on. In a blink, she reaches the other side. My sisters and I watch intently from the safety of Scylla. The hard-faced women share words with Lucinda and disappear beneath their deck. In exchange, a new form emerges, this one small. I squint, thinking it may be an illusion of distance, but hear Tahi and Dana whisper back and forth.

"She's but a child," Tahi says.

"Could it truly be?" Dana answers.

I draw as close as I dare to the banister, blocking the best of the sun's rays with my palm. They speak truth. No more than eight she must be, though clad in the finery of a captain, including a wide-brimmed hat. She stands with all the command a captain might have, all the formality of the hard-faced women. Her dirty blonde hair curls as it's whipped by the wind, and Lucinda bows before her.

"This is the advisor we seek?" I speak it aloud before I can think better of doing so.

"Only a child, surely." Tahi scoffs.

No sooner has the sound left Tahi's throat than Lucinda is waving us over. We look to one another, but before we can debate the safety of such an endeavor, Lily has climbed aboard the ladder and begun her crossing. Reginald, swollen and scabby, looks on from a shadow. Dana waves him back below deck.

All sisters follow suit, and I am last awaiting my turn on the ladder. I remove my boots for purchase, gripping the first wooden rung with my toes. A gust causes me to waver in my stance, but I right myself and cross with quick steps as I have watched my sisters do. The stern of the ship is entirely sunken, waves lapping about the mizzen. The trees we spotted at some distance loom even larger than they initially appeared, trunks thicker than two bodies pressed together. In their branches I hear birdsong, though I cannot spot the sopranos responsible for it. The entirety of the ship groans, a deep timbre that makes me think of longing and melancholy. Below deck must be entirely submerged, and I wonder whether the crew sleeps beneath starlight or within the gentle bosom of the sea.

Lucinda gathers us into a line. We face her and the child captain, a meter of height difference between them. Lucinda glides into an elegant curtsey, and in unison we do the same.

"I present to you my most trusted advisor. Eldest and wisest among us, you shall grant Captain Rose the highest respect."

"It is good you came to me." Rose speaks with perfect English diction, befitting of royalty. "Your captain has informed me of your trouble of late, and it is only through her wisdom that you may narrowly escape your collective downfall." Her doll-like eyes scan each of us. "Which among you is responsible for the human man who now infects your ship?"

Lily steps forward, eyes down.

"And what do you say to your sisters? How do you justify their endangerment?"

Lily tilts her chin upward and looks down upon Rose. My organs tighten. *Now is not the time for pride, Lily.*

"I say it was a bit of folly. I have never been one to deny myself what I fancy, and here is only one example amongst many." She glances back at us. "They could tell you as much. I shall not apologize for it. I am a woman of many desires, and I'll not be chastened or made smaller."

I brace. My line of sisters halts their breath.

"I admire your boldness," Rose says, the smallest smile cracking her lips. "Though in this case, it was ill advised." Rose pushes Lily back in line with a wave of her small hand. "Such an unnatural event as this has happened before, though not in many years. The harm already done cannot be reversed, though it can be slowed, and you need not suffer much more than you presently do." Rose walks the line of us, pausing a moment before each to inspèct. "I smell the pain on you. Already this man has infected you. Tell me." She stops before me, and I fear I may collapse under the weight of my fear. "What of *before* has returned to you?"

The eyes of my sisters press into me like hot coals. "Not much." My voice is a whine. "Only a time in the sea, just before Lucinda rescued us."

"Us?"

"Lily and I."

"Ah, you were together?" She takes a long breath through her nose. "Yes, that would explain the particular pain on you," she says in a low tone, as if speaking only to herself. "Sisters!" She projects with authority. "An endless present was gifted to you. The pain of your past was removed. And now by the folly of one amongst you, one of those gifts has been rescinded. But the other need not."

Lucinda's eyes are wide, as if she might see Rose's words hang upon the air.

"Rid yourself of this parasite in a way which honors your making, and the wound he caused will stop its hemorrhage. But I warn you, should you choose to let the memories of *before* guide you, your pain and emotions run wild, you may find your endless present revoked."

"What do you mean?" The voice comes from beyond my sight down our line, but I know, without looking, the pressing question comes from Lily's lips.

"What I mean, young lady, is should you travel as you plan to La Serenissima, you may find precisely what you are looking for. You may do just the thing you desire. And should you accomplish this aim, you will find yourself rotted beneath merciless waters. You may not, as you seem to so think, indulge your every whim, and be spared reasonable consequence."

Lucinda speaks with head bowed, "We shall dispatch the man with haste."

"You shall. On your own ship," Rose says. "You'll not expose my charges to his disease."

Lucinda nods and with that, Rose crosses the deck. Her feet splash as they hit the first of the steps leading to the submerged sleeping quarters. Undaunted by the water, she continues down them, the sea swallowing her small form and not a single bubble rising from her as she disappears beneath the lapping tide.

In her stead, the two hard-faced women return to join us. "We will offer you some company, since you have traveled all this way," one says to the group of us.

They prepare a fire circle, as is customary, and as they pile tinder upon a barrel, the tide rises to our knees. Tahi sits to my left and Dana beside her. To my right, Lily has perched upon some overturned crate. I sneak glances at her. There's no sorrow in her face, but a lick of frustration. There's a driving urge to take her into my arms, to coddle her. I know how it beguiles her when her hand is forced. I can only hope that this is the extent of the shadow upon her, that she does not harbor any fondness for Reginald, and that her commitment is solely to getting her own way, as it long has been, and not to the dragon Reginald himself.

As the sun melts into the horizon, we are bathed in orange light. Still, I've seen no passion in the faces of our hosts, merely duty. They sit beside one another just outside of our circle of sisters, as if waiting for the fire to die so they might retire to their watery beds. The raised pyre roars despite the rising water amongst us. The tide swirls our skirts about our ankles and sops our socks. Dalia tells a folktale of her people, the shadows exaggerating her features. Moryana watches eagerly, elbows perched upon her knees. There's a tickle about my ankle, which draws my gaze down. Just a brush of my pants, but beside me I notice Tahi's mottled flesh beneath the waterline. It's grey in the low light, but something draws my eye to her calf where two holes sit, dark as the surrounding water. I squint to see through the dusk, and though I expect a wave to shift or a flame to change the light and reveal it was just some illusion, the spots remain: twin boreholes the size of Ambrose's fangs. As I think to ask her about them, Dalia's voice raises and distracts me.

"Every year! As if they call us home, seeking penance, longing for their deaths!"

"In June you say?" Lily is transfixed. Unusual for her to be interested in anyone's story.

"It's why I so quickly agreed to change our course. La Serenissima has a fine coastline which will welcome us with open arms should we time our voyage precisely."

"And we might walk amongst them? On land?" Lily addresses Lucinda now, who smirks, her face bathed in shadow.

"Indeed. Each June, but only for the festival."

"We must go!" Lily reminds me of a child begging for a sweet.

"I had wished to surprise you all when I learned you desired to port there. But I suppose Dalia has unknowingly shed light on my little secret."

"They honor us!" Dalia says, her face full of joy.

There's a wild lightness about us, for this first time since Reginald joined our ranks.

"It will be so wonderful: to mingle amongst the crowds, inspect the goods of merchants, feed the stray cats. Captain, might we bring one aboard? I've longed for a companion!" Moryana is as happy as I've ever seen her.

Churning water and frantic splashes silence the discussion, and our collective eyes turn to our hosts. Their pallor has blanched, and one holds something with two hands. "I detest snakes," she says. With a twist of her wrist, a crack ripples through the night. There's a smack beside me, flesh against water, then the clatter of bones. Tahi's dress floats, seemingly empty. The thing inside my chest stops beating.

The woman who made the crack tosses a black-and-white snake into the roaring fire, where it drapes limply across two branches, a streak of vermillion leaking from its mouth.

Ambrose.

A spray of water hits my face and I turn to see Dana grasping and swiping frantically at Tahi's floating dress. In her clenched fists she holds bones, bleached and clean as if stripped of impurity by a thousand years.

"Tahi!" The name erupts from her lips and soars through the night sky. Shock lays heavy over the island ship. I watch my sisters flock to my side as if through a haze. My thoughts roll as if tossed by choppy seas. I retreat into myself, clench my eyes shut, and what I find there in the dark is Ambrose's spirit. He is kind enough, before he departs to the next realm, to impart the secret of Tahi's making, a story that causes the dangers of our memory to press even more fervently upon my mind.

CHAPTER TEN

Tahi's Tale:

As told by the spirit of Ambrose, the sea krait, his last act on this Earthly realm

I had just found a delightfully succulent crab. His sweet meat trailed through the tiny holes I punctured in his shell, and I was swallowing him up when there came a great disturbance at the shoreline. It annoyed me, that my first good meal in days had been disturbed by some oafish human, so I darted through the reef to investigate. Nestled between an anemone and a bit of fire coral, the vibrations of his booming voice made me draw back my lips and bare my teeth. Though I spoke the language, I could barely make out the words, so much vitriol was laced through them. This much I heard clearly.

"Useless! How many times have I—" I'll spare the rest of the words, for I'm sure you can imagine this man spewed every horrid word contained in his feeble mind at the poor woman (and to think they say *I* am venomous!). I came to see her face when he thrust it through the water's surface. Gaping were her eyes! How the saltwater must have burned them. I was struck by the art that adorned her face, beautiful, with her long dark hair swirling all around it, even as she drowned. Bubbles streamed from her mouth, and the ocean gobbled up most of her screams. He wrenched her up then, spewed more hatred. Up and down. It went on like this for some time: screams above, then bubbles below. Her lungs expanded and retracted as she tried to gasp for breath between the submersions. Until, finally, she gasped at just the wrong moment, drew a hefty helping of seawater into her lungs. There was a bit of thrashing. Sand rose in a flurry all around us and made it hard to see, but I felt enough vibration to know she moved about, a few last swipes at freedom, before her body went limp. You might think he would've just left her then, but no!

Her body left the water, water dripping back onto the surface like pouring rain. And then there was a great pressure and a tearing of my flesh. I lashed out, no fault of my own, to save myself. Sunk my fangs into a hunk of meat nearby. Her calf, it turned out. Beside me in the shallows, she died. A snake such as myself seldom feels regret, but in this case, I lingered near her. I hadn't meant to bring her to her end, and, after all, I was still hungry, despite the lovely crab meal I already mentioned. I thought I might snack a bit around the meatier parts of her. Waste not, want not, after all. But then the strangest thing happened.

When night turned the sky and ocean black, she woke! Her painted flesh was even more radiant under the moonlight. The patterns mixed with shadows of the clouds beneath the moon, and when she walked beneath the deep, heading toward open water, I abandoned my usual hunting ground in the shallows, compelled to follow her. I carried that compulsion ever after, following here, even to Scylla where you came to know me.

So you see, though I did not intend to, and though another would likely have caused her death in my stead, it was I who ended the mortal life of Tahi of Tonga. Remorseful as I have been, I was also entranced by her and wished to serve her. And so I have! A great many years. You yourself have benefitted from my presence. It is time I joined the eldest kraits which swim inside the night sky, but before I leave, I will make myself plain.

It is only through fulfilled purpose may you rest, be it vengeance or some other powerful thing. Your endless present is somewhat conditional. Should you and your sisters learn the truth of your deaths, and should those deaths be avenged, you may find rest as Tahi has. Though it will not be amongst me and my kind in the night sky, and also not so simple as an even exchange. Do with this what you will. I have never fully understood your kind.

Ambrose's spirit nuzzles my ear one last time.

"This is where I leave you, Jaq of Scylla. My twinkling brothers call from above, and it is high time I joined them."

With that, the spirit of Ambrose slithers into the crisp cool air. Only then do I become aware of the sobbing at my side, my sisters huddled in a writhing mass over Tahi's bones. Dana collects what remains of Tahi in her skirt, white as newly erupted teeth in the glistening moonlight. One by one we sisters scale the ladder back to Scylla. Sadness aches in our collective soul for the lost ones. Vengeance burns for a man named Reginald, left behind and sucking greedy breaths through his infectious nose.

Lucinda passes Lily and I, a stern look her only command. The others whisper curses under their breath in Lily's direction before retiring to their quarters under the guise of sleep. But they will not sleep. Not until what must be done is done. Wordless, Lily beckons me to follow. She winds through the forecastle, to a quiet place we seldom go.

She leans against a dive cage, a remnant of the foolish sailors who inhabited the ship before us, who thought such a thing might make them safe beneath blue waters. She folds her arms across her chest. "I will not do Lucinda's bidding."

A fragile hope snaps inside me like a wishbone. "Lily, why?" Unable to hide the pleading in my voice, I grasp her by the shoulders. "You've had your fun. I am in pieces, as you wished. Our sisters are in pieces! Is this not enough?"

She cracks a grin as a tear rolls down my cheek.

"Come." She takes me by the hand. "You really must spend some time with him."

I plant my feet where they stand and lean against her tugging.

"Jaq, come!"

As if I am some trained beast, I allow her to lead me down the steps. We pass what was once our room, quiet so the others don't hear us. When we reach the guest chambers, she turns the knob slowly and nudges the door with the tips of her fingers. It emits a long groan and reveals Reginald sprawled upon the bed, sheets twisted amongst his legs.

"Touch him," she whispers. Her eyes are aflame.

I recoil, step backward into the hall. "I will not."

"Touch him!" It's a hiss. "Touch him and you will see."

She yanks at my shirt and I take stumbling steps into the room. Another groan tells me she has shut the door behind me, but my eyes are fixed upon this man, this monster, whose chest rises and falls, unaware of a predator's watchful eyes upon him. My lids close with the sensation of breath on my neck and arms encircling me from behind. Lily caresses the inside of my shoulder, to my elbow, to my wrist. Like the jaws of a mother cat upon her baby's neck, she guides my movement. My eyes snap open. She holds my hand above a bit of bare skin on Reginald's calf.

Touch him. It is as if Lily beckons me from within my own mind. Compelled, from within and without, the wiry hairs of his leg make contact with my thumb.

In a flash, I am transported through time. I stand amongst a bustling crowd in a busy market. A butcher attempts to persuade me to purchase the loin over the shank, but his words are white noise as Lily grins at me from the bread stand. Her flashing eyes invite me to follow her, and searing pain—

I shake myself loose from Lily's hold, and nearly topple over in my haste to distance myself from Reginald's flesh.

A rustling of sheets tells me he's waking.

"Your envy blinds you to the gifts of his touch, Jaq."

She places a bare foot upon the bed. Reginald wipes the sleep from his eyes and raises himself to a sitting position. "Would you not cast your jealousies aside and join us?"

As the dragon Reginald realizes his circumstance, he puffs his chest in a manner most excited and revolting. My jaw hangs and I shake my head as he runs his hands up her legs beneath her skirt, as she tosses her head back and closes her eyes. A soft moan escapes her lips as his hand disappears between her thighs, and though I thought my heart had already broken, it finds new places to shatter, and must now be reduced to dust.

Just as I fear I will be reduced to hysterics, Lily jolts upright. Startled, Reginald withdraws his sickly hands from her perfect form.

"You." Her voice is a sharpened sword. Lily's limbs go rigid as if she is possessed by some demonic force. Her skin alights with a greenish hue. "Follow me."

She rises from the bed, Reginald following as if she is some pied piper, and I trail the both of them. Lily retraces the way we came, through the foremast, back to the tucked away spot where the dive cage rests.

She clasps his face in her hands. "It is time for a swim." Her eyes are so near his own, he must see nothing but them. "The cage will keep you safe." Eyes vacant, he nods.

The metal screams as he drags the cage across the deck to the starboard side. Lily tells me her plan in hushed tones, lips dancing just beyond the reach of my own. My desire thrums. A tiny fire is lit which has not burned since that first day I spotted him at sea. I gaze up at celestial bodies for confirmation. Yes, Cassiopeia shines bright. My lover is returning to me.

I can scarcely contain my fervor as I affix ropes to the steel bars. I glance beyond the banister. Beneath, the waters are calm as a frozen lake. A briny sheet of glass awaits us, possibilities endless below. A nudge of not half my strength, and the cage careens over the side. I secure the rope to the main mast, such that half the cage is submerged and half glitters with starlight.

I don't know what spells Lily whispers to him, but Reginald crosses the deck with eagerness. *What promise have you made, dear Lily?* I see my own enchantment in his glazed, pitiful eyes. But we are not the same. The distance between us is that of predator and prey.

Clothed in her thin shift, a gentle wind ripples the sheer fabric as Lily steps a graceful foot upon the banister and hoists herself upon it. She outstretches her arms like some exotic bird. A quick glance at Reginald, and she clasps her hands above her head, hair coiling and uncoiling in the night wind. She dives.

Reginald runs to the place from which she leapt. She bobs beside the cage, still only half submerged. Gripping the bars, she leans back and dips her ashen hair into the black deep. She swishes her head back and forth, beckoning Reginald to join her. He tears his shirt from his chest with such force a button pings off and strikes my arm. His zeal for death impresses me.

Reginald's body breaks the water with a great splash. When the froth clears, Lily is helping him inside the cage. He reaches for her arm to ease her inside with him, but she evades him. With a flick of two fingers, she signals me. I untie my first set of knots, and the cage drops a meter. Now only glimpses of the bars can be seen above the water's surface. Reginald presses his mouth to the air. Even from the distance, I see his tongue flick in and out as he slurps at life.

It is my time.

I leap from the banister and enter the water with the smallest splash. Saltwater welcomes me like a home.

Beneath, I seek out Lily's form. Her white shift is near translucent, soaked through and through. I swim to her like a creature of the deep. It has been so long since I've seen her true form. Even through the darkness, I make out the flesh hanging in ribbons, the color of midnight just below her shift. I long to touch her, to caress the shreds of her decay. But our work is not done.

Reginald grasps the top bars with both hands, face pressed to the air. He's murmuring something, a muddled version of *too deep*, but I can't take my eyes off Lily. Beneath the lapping waves, she twists her body to the rhythm of the ocean. Clinging to a vertical bar with one arm, she tosses herself this way and that, hair—even longer beneath than above—swaying about her. In her face are many crevasses, all the beauty of an ancient ice shelf, worn by time and flowing water. Though her nose has worn away, her lips gone, exposing orderly rows of white teeth, she is my Lily. I desire to hold her close to me.

Reginald's curiosity overtakes him, and with a gulp of breath he plunges his head underwater to look for his traitorous love. He must see her truly now, for his eyes grow wide despite the burn of the salinity. He bangs his head on the top bars in his haste to return to the world of air. Shrieking overtakes the night's quiet, and I find myself at Lily's side. She looks upon me, laces her skeletal fingers in mine. Our reunion. At last.

"You lied," Lily says to him, submerged up to her lips. "All the while you knew me. Coveted me. Watched me from afar as I went about my daily tasks in another life. *I remember.*"

"Long I have loved you, Lilith." Reginald has never been so pale, so impotent. "You love me too. I have seen it!"

Lily's smile is cold.

"I came to save you, to free you from the evil magic's hold. Don't you see? It was you I sought! Long months at sea—"

"Say my name," Lily whispers.

Reginald responds with a plea to the uncaring night. "Rusalka." The word dies as Lily's hand plunges through the bars, and though Reginald tries his best to move out of reach, her fingers find his ribcage. As they wriggle, horror and shock turn to involuntary laughter, escaping his mouth in streams and globs of mirror-shine bubbles. Fire courses through me, a calling of the oldest gods, and I plunge my hands between the bars as well, seeking out ribs and underarms and squeezing where his thigh meets his knees. In his hysterics, he pours his bubbles into our mother, the endless sea.

Lily tickles.

I tickle.

A sweet and lovely thing.

When the last, slim trail of air escapes Reginald's lips, he sucks in, filling his lungs with a most inhospitable substance. His final moments bring forth the beasts within. Our girlish fingers turn once more to blades, carving flesh and muscle and sinew from his bones. The water is stained with him, a thicker, more murky black as we rend him from himself. Once more I find myself in a trance, more animal than Jaq. My need, my craving, my desire seizes full control. When finally it peaks, I am sated. Lily climbs atop the cage and I follow. We look up, once again restored to our earthly beauty by the night air. Lucinda gazes down from above. Her flesh as deep and lovely as the night sky, her smile as brilliant as the twinkling stars. Without a single grunt of effort, she pulls the rope, ferrying Lily and I back aboard Scylla, Reginald's bones in tow within the bars of the dive cage.

CHAPTER ELEVEN

Lucinda takes her leave of us, bones of Reginald in her long arms, and retires to the captain's quarters to do what she will. Unbeknownst to her, I ferret away the bits of him I most desire—a full set of his teeth.

Hair streaming saltwater, clothes sopping over goosed skin, Lily whispers, "Take me." And now I will do what I might, what I have longed to do. Taking hurried steps, her hand in mine, we flee the deck for the privacy of our bed. The door has barely settled on its hinges when Lily frees her body from the translucent shift. Water beads in the bones around her shoulders, falls like raindrops over her hardened nipples. With no boots to remove, I make quick work of sliding off my pants and undergarments. My shirt, a smart thing with a long line of buttons, is a different matter. Lily's feet slap the wood floor as she crosses the room and yanks at the fabric. Buttons pop in quick succession, go pinging across the floor, bouncing about the walls. She presses her naked bosom to mine, her breasts firm and far larger than my own, create a pool between our bodies, catching drops that trail from my hair and the tip of my nose.

I tilt her chin with a curved finger. Her lilac eyes meet mine. The softness of her lips threatens to swallow me whole, and, without thought, I have lifted her, am carrying her to the bed. I toss her upon it, her fall cushioned by throw pillows. On my hands and knees, I crawl upon her, resting my body on hers. Our tongues intermingle in a fine ballet. Her fingers on my back. Her nails digging in. I wrap her leg around my torso, position myself at just the right angle to feel her with the most intimate parts of myself. She's slick, as am I. The rub of her flesh on my own intoxicates me. I close my eyes, luxuriating in the exquisite pleasure.

A whisper in my ear. "Look at me."

My lids snap open. Her gaze catapults me backward through time, into memory long forgotten.

Another place.

The same eyes.

Another life, but the same Lily.

Jaq Before

Afternoon light pushes through the window. Dust hangs in the air, caught in the beams that pour through the sheer curtains. Lily is beneath me, leg wrapped around, my torso pitched at the perfect angle for my sex to meet hers. My fingers cover her mouth, stifling her moans. She licks at them, feral with need beneath me. I direct my huffing breaths into the pillow, knowing the farmhand is just outside. Fearing the danger should he hear us.

Lily tilts her hips and bucks up against me. Her eyes roll with pleasure. She is close. Hands searching my backside, her breaths hitch in my ear. A moan and a curse. Nails in my flesh. Her climax drags me into mine, a few quick strokes and I reach my precipice, collapsing into her. We linger there, catching our breath.

"I think he's beginning to suspect," she says, her voice hoarse.

My guts clench with the insinuation. I roll off her. "And what would you have think that?"

Outside, a rooster crows. "Get dressed." She hops up, unashamed of her nakedness, beckoning me to do the same.

I abide. My pants lay in a heap at the bedside. I untangle them, free my undergarments, and begin to slide them over my legs when heavy footsteps careen down the hall.

"Jaqueline!" A furious male voice down the hall.

No.

My husband's voice.

"The window!"

Lily's eyes are wide with fear. She glances to the window, painted shut, as the steps draw closer.

"Jaqueline!"

Her purple dress is twisted amongst her arms as she fumbles with it.

"Quickly," I plead.

She shakes it, slips her legs through the skirt when the door flies open.

"I knew it!" His voice booms, echoing off the dusty glass window. Lily yanks at her dress, just gets it over her belly when he delivers a smack across my cheek. "Whore!"

My face flushes scarlet. My ears ring.

"There were whispers about you in town. Your *unnatural predilections.*" Spittle mists my eye. "But I refused to believe it. Had to see it with my own eyes."

Lily slips her arm through one of the straps when he grabs her by the arm. "No, leave it. Let them see you! Let the whole town see who you truly are."

Edward drags her. I'm able to shimmy on my pants and grab a shirt in one hand before they clear the bedroom. I hear myself begging him to stop. His arm shakes with rage as he pulls her over our threshold onto the dirt road. Her dangling earrings clatter together, the only sound but for his thundering footsteps as he makes his way to the town's square. A merchant stares from his bread stand, loaf of sourdough held aloft. Still, I hear myself screaming. A woman with an armful of cut flowers stops mid-stride, foot hovering above the ground as Lily sobs. But Edward is blind to all but his mission. We pass the blacksmith, who shushes a horse spooked by the commotion. So many eyes upon us, and not a single hand to help. When finally he reaches the square, he throws Lily to the ground. I stumble over myself to reach her, shielding her from anticipated blows with my body.

Edward clears his throat.

"I have found, in my own bed chambers, those among us who would serve devils."

Surely this is but a dream, I think. But the bruise on Lily's shoulder is already forming, skin tinged green by strong fingers.

"It fills me with shame to think upon how I heard your whispers, and yet denied this truth until my own sight confirmed it. *Unnatural* women defile us with their transgression. They make a mockery of our sacred marital vows. They warp tradition, the noble pleasure of the bedchamber, with their filth."

A goat bleats from a distance. The town holds its breath.

"There is but one thing to be done, and to reclaim what remains of my honor, I shall do it myself, before you all as witnesses."

Lily's cries have quieted. Eyes puffy, she looks to him with the face of a woman who has tasted something sour.

"Edward, please!" The pitch of my voice makes a nearby mother usher her children inside a shop, but my plea only incites him. As if lifted by a creature from lore, I am once again on my feet, Lily's amber hair obscuring my vision. But I know we draw closer to the sea. The scent of brine fills the air, the gentle rush of water in the shallows.

"There's but one thing to do with impurity," Edward says. He pushes me into a tide pool, slick stones breaking my fall. When I wipe the water from my eyes, he holds Lily by the hair. "Wash it out."

He plunges her face beneath the surface. Bubbles stream up all around her, tossing her hair about. I dig my fingernails into his wrist, attempt to rip his hands away, but it's no use. I cry out.

"Please! Help, anyone!" But none come to our aid.

Lily's arms flail. Edward's eyes bulge, his face the color of pain. Time slows then, just for a moment. Lily relaxes. I think I detect her lavender scent. Edward releases his grip, eases her body into the water. She floats. Like a goddess, she floats. Tears cascade down my cheeks, and the Adriatic Sea becomes imperceptibly deeper as they join with the froth. There's a particular pair of eyes I hope cannot see this, though, I cannot recall who they belong to. This moment spans a thousand years, is gone before I can hold it.

I don't see what kills me.

There's a loud crack of my skull, and my blood turns the tide pool the color of the sky after a storm. Our bodies float together, Lily's and mine. Some townspeople come to look. A woman holds her skirt and steps barefoot into the shallows, covers her mouth when she spots the gore. Two men slosh into the tide pool, soaking their boots. They mutter back and forth about worthiness before deciding to have an ale. A child stumbles upon us, chasing an errant, wooden ball through the street. He lingers longest, eyes searching us like puzzle pieces. Then, quietly, he goes.

Night falls.

We begin to bloat.

No stars penetrate the blackness, no moon. Sadness hangs in the sky as fog. Our bodies drift. By the machinations of some divine or ghoulish being, we remain together, even as our corpses open and release gasses. Even as we sink to the sugar sand bottom. The current fails to find the strength to tear us apart. Love, or some inversion of it, has bound us, even in death. So, when we wake, sometime later on, at the bottom of the sea, coupled we remain.

I know not how the final bit of knowledge comes to me, perhaps a gift from the spirit of Ambrose, my spy. But sure as I had witnessed it with my own eyes, I know a final watcher visits our seaside graves. Long he stares at the black rolling waves, searching them for our bodies, for Lily's body. But already we are gone, as our mother, Adriana, intended. When finally he abandons his macabre quest, the moonlight illuminates his face. The younger face of a dragon named Reginald.

I return, trembling, to the present.

"Did you … did you see it too?"

Lily's hand upon my shoulder tells me she has.

"This is why …" Of course. Lily discovered Reginald's stalking just as she intended to bed him before my eyes. Revenge the true reason for her willingness to dispatch him. A sharp mixture of guilt and shame and rage makes a potent cocktail in my marrow. "So this is why we must go." Not a question, but an answer. "To La Serenissima."

Lily nods. "Her shores have yanked at me, and it becomes clearer why with every hint of *before*. It was our home, once."

The truth of it fortifies me. "And when we get there?"

"More shall be revealed. Of this much I trust."

I think of Rose. "What of the small captain's warning?" Her words repeat in my head as an echo. *Should you travel as you plan to La Serenissima, you may find precisely what you are looking for. You may do just the thing you desire. And should you accomplish this aim, you will find yourself rotted beneath merciless waters.*

"Rotted beneath merciless waters we are already," Lily says. Her irises turn the cold color of tide pools. "We've dealt with Reginald, whose leering eyes and treacherous tongue betrayed our secret. I wish to return to dear Edward, to pay him the same kindness he so tenderly bestowed upon me."

CHAPTER TWELVE

By the time we reach La Serenissima, all the pigs are dead. They lie in a heap, a halo of buzzing flies around the mess. More proof, though none was needed, that Reginald's appetite could not match our own. Yinka will be sad to hear. Perhaps I'll keep it from her. Scylla tips and rights herself as the anchor is tossed overboard. The deck vibrates with activity, beneath the only respite from my sisters, circling and mumbling their histories, plans for vengeance.

Once more I visit Yinka. Though her dress is more soiled, her eyes perhaps more sunken, she looks much the same as the day she was caged.

"How many days, Yinka?" My fingertips caress the bars, the rusty keyhole.

"Один или сто,[4]" she replies, head in her hands.

"Has anyone told you of Ambrose? Of Tahi?"

She nods. Her eyes well with melancholy and a touch of something which does not belong—envy perhaps.

"So it would seem that with the death of our maker, we too finally find rest."

---

[4] One or one hundred

Her posture straightens. "How then, shall I find my end?" English words from her lips once again ignite a flame of hope for her recovery. "Shall I strike down the lake? Drain it perhaps? Or was it the cold which was responsible? Which among you would avenge me to the cold? Would you set the whole world ablaze to do it?"

My heart sinks. I realize in an instant that Yinka is right. How might her tragedy be avenged? Ambrose did say it was not so simple. A mystery perhaps Lucinda could solve.

"It's not as straightforward as you would make it seem. For how old is our captain? Surely any mortal responsible for her death has long since met their demise, would they not? Yet still she sails. There is more to our making than you see, more to our unmaking than you understand."

Her red hair hangs limp about her ears. She twists a few strands and bites at her lip.

"There must be a way for me to join him. I grow tired, Jaq."

There are no portholes in the brig, but suddenly my mind shifts to the scene which must lie outside. If only Yinka could see it. "A trip ashore might do you well, sister."

"Ashore?"

"Aye. A party just for us. In our honor, so Lucinda says."

Yinka smooths her hair back as if she's expecting company. "I wouldn't mind a trip ashore, yes." Biting her cheek within her mouth she says, "Will you speak with our captain on my account? Tell her as much?"

"I will."

Her mood improved, I leave the brig, intent on following through with my promise. The shore will do us all some good. Many years we have lived on swells at the mercy of the wind. Stable ground would be a welcome change for us all. I cross the ship and find Lucinda in her quarters, door ajar. I rap upon it thrice.

"Come in, Jaq," she says without looking up from her desk. She studies a leather-bound book, an ancient volume from the look of it.

"I come to speak with you."

"Yes, so I assumed."

I step inside, close the door gently behind me. "Our answers as of late have raised more questions in my mind."

"And for me as well." She turns a page, eyes tight to the words scrawled in a language in which I am inept.

"What has happened to Tahi?"

At last she meets my eyes. "Tahi rests."

"Aye, but where? And for what reason?"

Lucinda pulls in a long, ceremonious breath, for our lungs are long useless. "We are born of tragedy and great emotion and water. This much I am certain. How we meet our end though ..." She shakes her head as if a thought has escaped her. "Of this I am less sure."

"Before he—well, you will think it a flight of fancy. But Ambrose, after his neck was snapped, whispered to me that should our deaths be avenged, we find our rest. A second death, perhaps, as it were."

"Aye, this is so." Her lips become a tight line.

"But what then of Yinka? Whose accidental death leaves no perpetrator behind? No evil mortal to stalk and kill? And—"

"And what of those of us whose killers long since met their own end," she finishes.

"Aye. What of you?"

She returns her attention to the book. "I seek these answers just as you do, Jaq. The old ways are not so easily understood. But do heed Rose's words." She rises from her seat and seems taller than ever as she approaches me and places her hand upon my shoulder. "I offer you endlessness. Eternity with your love. Would you so quickly toss that away for a moment of vengeance?"

Lucinda smells of bergamot and fresh linen. I think of Edward's vicious hand upon Lily's head, the last bubbles streaming from her submerged mouth. My belly roils with need for retribution. But then I think of emptiness. Of whatever loneliness might await me should I find rest. Most certainly Lily would not be there. And a shot of cold runs through my spine. "I would not lightly throw away the gift you bestowed upon us."

"The gift was not mine to bestow. I merely granted you a home, so you need not wander the sea beds. Introduced you to your sisters, so you need not find yourself without family. You are now, as you have ever been while under my charge, free to do as you might. I will not cage you as I have Yinka. Her restraints only exist to keep her from acting recklessly and without proper understanding of what her actions might bring. I will release her to go ashore with the lot of you. I know this question also weighed on your mind when you entered my chamber. So there is your answer. Yinka will do what she might, knowing fully that the seafloor holds no reunion for her. That her brother does not wait for her there."

I flash my captain a questioning look.

"As I have said, there is little that occurs aboard Scylla of which I am unaware. Seek your freedom from this world, if you will."

Freedom. I roll the word over in my mind. What might freedom mean, except the possibility of being separated from Lily? Why would I desire that?

"Lily's eyes are set on revenge. I fear there will be no stopping her."

Lucinda *hmphs.* "Lily's will has ever been outside of my purview."

"But if she has her revenge, then my killer is also extinct. So she might decide for us both."

"I suspected that might be the case. Talk to your lover. See what agreement you might reach, about living or dying or resting or sailing. Remember, the world is full of many violent men who you might drown with all the lust and fervor you so enjoy, but whose end would not parse you from us, or from one another. Whatever you choose, you have my blessing."

Lucinda eases open her desk drawer and draws from it an iron key. I receive it from her.

"For Yinka. Please ensure she understands."

"I shall." With a tip of my head, I take my leave of her. My steps are weighty down the dim hall, the iron key heavy in my pocket and the gravitas of the decision before me clawing at my mind. I elect to free Yinka before I speak with Lily, but as I pass our open door, she calls me from inside.

"We've arrived in port, lover." She is perched upon the edge of the bed, wearing only a bodice. Her waist is cinched by corset strings, and her hair hangs loose, spiraling around her ample chest. Lily leans forward, welcoming me to take full view of her beauty. It is outside of my ability to deny her. No will of my own, I am before her, looking down on her form.

"Lily—"

"Shhhh." She presses a single finger to my lips. "Let us not debate the merits of this life. Have we not sailed many years? The pleasures of the world have been our own, and now we might enjoy the most singularly delicious thing, a death avenged."

The draw burns within me with all the glory of a rising sun. I place my hands upon her shoulders. Light trickles in our circular window, dances upon her hair, now white from salt and sun. "I do not wish to be parted from you." The words are too true. They pull sorrow from my heart.

"Ah, but think of it, Jaq! Think of Edward, eyes bulging, face the same shade of violet as the dress I drowned in. Imagine his cries, his pleas for mercy, and the ecstasy of granting him none."

It plays before my eyes like a vision. I admit, the thought quickens my pulse. The black blood or wickedness that flows within me races about my extremities, settles in a place between my legs. "It would be …"

"The crowned jewel of our living." Her purple eyes burn gold. Such rich fire within them. Wrapping her arms around my waist, she presses the iron key and draws it from my pocket.

"For Yinka."

Lily dangles the key ring aloft. "Yes," her voice is a hiss. "Let us free our sister. Let us see what trouble her sadness might bring to the men who walk about on land."

Yinka's freedom comes not as a gush, but a trickle. She pads from her cell, back hunched, shielding her eyes as they adjust to the change in light in the hall. Her voice is slender as a mouse when she excuses herself to tidy up in her quarters. Before she can depart us, I remind her, "Dimitri is not in the sea. You know this, yes?"

She nods, her eyes as large as a child's, and closes her chamber door behind her.

Lily grabs my hand. "Let's get to deck. I long to see *land*."

I don't know what I expected to see, but the busyness which greets me upon our deck causes my head to swoon. Ships! Not one, faint against a horizon line, but many! They fly flags of varying colors, have names all their own. Distant voices, *male* voices, ride upon the breeze, and most startling of all is the harbor. Men carry nets, roll barrels, chop heads off fish. Children scurry in the shallows, mothers chiding them from the safety of shore. There are shops! Houses! Chimneys emit smoke. Confronted by the chaos of life, the fullness of it, I grip Lily tightly as an anchor.

She shakes loose of my hold. Drawn to the port side like a flying bug to fire, she hops upon the banner, holding a bit of rigging to steady herself before I can stop her.

"Look at them," she says, eyes gaping. She reaches into the air as if to collect them in her palm. "So many."

Slowly, so as not to startle her, I approach. I place a steadying hand upon the small of her back. "They string banners—"

"For us."

Across a dirt road, amongst a smattering of merchant shops, a painted sign reads, *Green Week*.

"It is as Lucinda said." Lily's skirts billow in a strong gust. I hold her with both hands now, fear snaking up within me that she might fall to the depths below. "They welcome us. Invite their deaths with offerings of gaiety and ale." A giggle comes from a dark place inside her. She swings on the rigging, turning a full circle with reckless haste and faces me. "I shall bring it to them, Jaq." Her curled lips show long incisors. "Long have I collected my anguish, stacked my rage into neat piles and sorted it. My list of grievances is written in blood. I shall grant them each their wishes, show them the true nature of my *unnatural predilections*."

CHAPTER THIRTEEN

Lucinda calls us to order, demanding even Moryana come down from the crow's nest to receive instruction. We gather, feeling an extra bit of wind in the spot where Tahi should be. In a circle we sit, no pile of offerings in the center this time, and our captain paces around us with measured steps.

"Tomorrow brings June. You must remain upon Scylla until then. Our kind is not welcomed upon land until the morning's first light. Though I suggest you bide your time until the festivities are in full swing to make your approach. Suspicious eyes will less likely find you, should you disperse yourselves amongst a heavy crowd."

Lily is beside me, her gaze fixed on the distant lights of town.

"They are half expecting you, half believe you to be myth. In their hearts they know you to be real, and so throw this festival yearly in an attempt to appease you. The children will know you for what you are, but fear not. Their mothers and fathers will dismiss their childlike observations as fantasy. I will not join you ashore. And when the week comes to a close, I shall sail Scylla into the safety of deep waters. Those aboard shall be my crew. Should you choose to remain here and seek your vengeance with the one who most deserves it, remember to return to water at week's end. Else it shall claim you by force."

Dana speaks up, her sandy hair fastened in a braid so tight it seems to pry her eyes open. "Might we sail east next? I wish to find my father and repay him for my premature death."

"Yes!" Dalia says. "And then south! So I might find the man who stank of whiskey."

"East first," Moryana says through gritted teeth. "My cousin has walked freely for far too long. I should amend that, and quickly."

Lucinda extends an open palm. "Sisters, Scylla will ferry you to wherever your fiery hearts lead. Worry not. If retribution you seek, I shall play my part to ensure you have it."

Moryana presses her knuckles which crack one by one. "Then La Serenissima shall make a fine venue at which to practice my craft."

Yinka alone speaks not of revenge. She twists her red hair around her finger until the tip changes color.

Moryana's foot taps, leg jostles. She takes a swift breath and says, "Why should we wait 'til morning? They rest helpless in their beds." She jumps to her feet. "I wish to get an early start." Before Lucinda can speak a word, Moryana sprints toward the port side and dives over the banister. My sisters and I scurry to the railing and find her swimming with the swiftness of a rising tide.

"Should we—" Dana begins to ask, but Lucinda cuts her off.

"No need."

Waves churn around Moryana, and she ducks beneath white caps, pushed at an angle by the current, but continues toward the rocky shoreline.

"Will she—" Dalia starts, silenced by Lucinda's hand.

"Watch."

Moryana reaches the shallows and stands, black hair, black dress sopping into waist-deep water. She grabs her skirts and hikes them up, step by step drawing nearer to the empty shore. We hold our collective breath. The water licks at Moryana's ankles. She's a black spot against black night as her leg extends to take its place on shore, when a wave rises above the others. It reaches for her like the arm of a god, wraps itself around her leg. She turns, fear about her face, as another wave reaches and yanks her body back into the sea. The ocean churns. Wave after rolling wave spins her in a torrent. Her arms flail as she tries to regain her footing, but her strength is nothing against the fierceness of Adriana, our mother. The sea spits Moryana out, like an errant bit of bone in a fine steak, one hundred yards from the shoreline. Her head dips beneath the ocean's surface, and she rises once more, smoothing her black hair out of her face, before swimming back toward Scylla.

"As I told you," Lucinda says finally. "We wait until the first light of morning."

Dalia casts a rope to Moryana below, who scales it skillfully, showing all the practice her station in the crow's nest has afforded her. Her pale skin glistens in the moonlight, casting a faint greenish hue I've never before seen. When she has rejoined us on the main deck, trailing puddles of seawater, Lucinda summons us back into our circle.

"We shall not waste our night together. There's no promise we will be joined again once you breach the shores tomorrow. Let us take one another's hands."

Moryana's palm is clammy and cold. I warm it with my own. Lily sits across from me, joining with Dana and Dalia. Yinka takes my other palm. Heads bowed, Lucinda goes on.

"We invoke the blessings of our eldest gods. May we fulfill our purposes, should they be justice or joy." From a satchel at her side, Lucinda pulls a small object. It's matte white, the color of ivory. She passes it to Lily, draws forth another, and passes this to Dana. One by one she hands them out, and when I receive mine, I recognize it as a comb carved of bone.

"Fasten these into your hair before you go ashore. They shall hold the moisture of our mother sea, and in this way, you shall travel in the company of Adriana, mother to us all."

Yinka flips the comb over in her hand, runs her fingers along its pointed teeth. "And it will keep us safe?" There's pungent fear on her breath.

"From some things." Lucinda pats her shoulder as one might soothe a fussy infant.

An infant. The thought spurs a stitch of pain. Though why, I know not.

"Rest now. Dream of your intentions. There's no need to cover your heads tomorrow, nor secure your hair into pleats. All the town's women will allow their mane to flow freely, both to honor you and to camouflage you in the crowd. Whether they know it or not, they too seek your vengeance, though perhaps not with the same ferocity."

Moryana's walk to her chambers is a loud one, dress still trailing seawater and bare feet smacking upon wood.

The rest of us follow her, the quiet rife with intention and plans. Lily's movements beside me hold all the eagerness of a mare in heat. She takes two steps for every one needed, whips her head around at the slightest noise as if inviting a squabble. The whites of her eyes light our way to the bedchamber.

I think of my captive sailors, likely sleeping in my glass bottle, tucked away safely in my drawer. I envy them for a moment. Their guaranteed future together that none might rip away.

Though my mind is elsewhere when I slip beneath the sheets, Lily is alive with the promise of revenge. Eyes aflame, she mounts me, tears open my shirt. She grates her fingernails over my bare breasts and belly. I should revel in the perfection of her touch, should savor these sweet moments of lust with my truest love, but fear holds me from the fullness of pleasure. In one smooth motion, she lifts her dress over her head. White hair frames her face, eyes fixed on me. I grip her thighs as they straddle me, just my trousers and her undergarments separate us from one another. She rocks back and forth upon me, in time with the rolling sea, pressing the fabric to the center of my lust.

I've half a mind to stop her. To redress myself and insist instead on a conversation. To weigh pros and cons of—

She slides down, pressing her body flat to mine like an eel. Further she slithers, until I feel her hot breath through the fabric of my pants. She frees my button from its catch, and I arch my back, allowing her to slip off my pants and undergarments in a simple motion.

"Lily."

It's meant to give her pause, but my voice is a throaty whisper that sounds more like encouragement than anything else. Hooking her thumbs through her final piece of clothing, she wiggles her hips and frees her nakedness from the binds of clothing.

All but her splendor disappears from my mind. *What if this is the last time? I should savor it, should I not?*

She parts my legs with a nudge inside my thighs. So rarely does she take this position, I spread myself eagerly before her. The wetness and warmth of her tongue glides from my knee, up the inside of my thigh.

"I wish to consume you," she whispers between my legs, as if not for my ears but for my—

Her lips are upon me, soft as a pounding heart. Her mouth circles, easing my eyes shut. Delicious pressure starts from a corner then builds to the place I desire it most. I find I am leaning into her, pressing myself to her mouth. Muscles clench at my center. My fingers tangle in her hair. I have nearly reached my limit when the warmth stops.

A breath of cold.

"Would you deny us our retribution, lover?" she asks, her face slick with me.

"No!" It comes out a breathy, high pitch.

A smile curls her lips and her head sinks once more. It takes only a few strokes of her tongue to make me cry out.

Panting, I feel her scaling my body once more. And when I open my eyes, she hovers just above me. A tear runs down my cheek, and she catches it with a delicate finger.

"Don't despair, Jaq." She pushes my long hair to one side and rubs the shaved side of my head. "Many years we have traveled in purgatory. We ascend to our purpose at last, come what may."

She plants a kiss upon my forehead. Perhaps Lily is right. As wise Yinka once said, all good things die. Only poison is forever. And there is always a chance that our rest might include one another. Thus far naught has had the strength to separate us. So why might one final death?

CHAPTER FOURTEEN

Hair loose, combs fastened, my sisters and I take turns descending a rope to pile into our row boat. The morning hangs heavy with mist, obscuring our encroachment upon the shore. Lucinda watches from the bow, wishing us fulfilled purpose with a wave of her hand.

I fiddle with my ship in a bottle, unseen beneath my coat. When I stashed it away before Lily woke, I knew not whether it was to bring some piece of home to this strange place, or to bring something strange with me home. Nevertheless, it is a small comfort to know my insect sailors make this adventure with me. In my pocket I harbor a full set of dragon's teeth, a steadying reminder of my power.

Moryana rows, her black hair whipped straight by the wind. Her emerald dress gleams, the sheen of expensive fabric drawing warmth from her pale skin. Yinka wears blush skirts, her red hair flaming, comb tucked in at the crown. Lily wears purple, rich in tone as the one she died in. Her locks, which I'm now convinced were bleached by pervasive memory, are so white as to give off the slightest green hue. I wear pants and a brown leather vest, most practical for travel.

Only a few bodies move about the dock. A man rolls a barrel. Another fiddles with a crab trap. Banners strung the night before wave pastel silks from high above the streets, affixed to clothing lines and hung in a zigzagging pattern. Moryana steers us to a small cove concealed by birch trees. Fog drifts off the water, and if I knew no better, I would think we emerged from some swamp. When we hit the loamy soil, Dana hops out and drags our small boat ashore.

I can speak not for the others, but when my boots rest on stable ground, there's a quickening within. The dull ache of anger that ever pulsed aboard Scylla has sharpened to points. It rakes at me like fingernails upon my neck. I thirst.

"I think I'd like to return to the ship," Yinka says, the last remaining in her seat.

"With these scrawny arms?" Dalia pinches her shoulder. "You wouldn't clear the halfway mark."

Yinka looks to me, and Lily must feel her pleading eyes upon me because she pulls me toward her by my waist. "You'll have to wait," she says. "Enjoy what you will, be it sobbing lonely in the woods rather than staring upon open waters, or whatever it is you might enjoy."

Yinka casts her eyes down and twists her blush skirts around her freckled arms. I extend my hand, which she accepts, and help her from the boat. Moryana stashes our vessel beneath some fallen branches.

"We should stay together," she says. "At least for a time."

It feels not like a homecoming. Rather, I feel a stranger in this land. My free-flowing hair tickles my neck like spider's legs, and I fasten it into a bun as we walk, using my comb as a pin. Few words are exchanged, palpable tension in the air slowing our steps. When the trees thin, Moryana pauses. My sisters and I follow suit. Voices echo through the dirt road ahead, talking of fish and cheese and wine.

Dalia speaks in a hushed tone. "We should call out to our cousin, the Lesovik. Ask for his blessing over our pursuits." Nods of agreement lead to collection of goods. Dana traps a chicken who's wandered too far from her brood. Moryana assembles sticks into a small pyre. I push dust into piles around it. Lily tugs out a few of Yinka's hairs.

"Ouch!"

And smiles at her pain.

I gain a sense that inside my hidden bottle, the insect sailors sing a song of protection. For themselves or for my sisters, I know not. Old magic sizzles in the air as Moryana snaps the chicken's neck.

"We offer this gift unto you, Lesovik."

Lily ties Yinka's hairs around its broken neck and lays it upon the pyre. She whispers something into its unhearing ear. A thin voice reaches across a distant realm to deliver a message: *Wait here.*

I inform the others. After some arguing from Dalia and Moryana, who wish to begin their destruction posthaste, we agree to settle in the shadows until dusk and heed the warning of the old god.

This decision was best, I think. By the time the sun shoots orange streaks through the sky, the dirt road has filled with sweaty faces and merriment. Bodies press against one another as they pass, so little room in the street. Mothers lead their children to an early bedtime, then return to the street, ale in hand. Once clear voices begin to slur. Kind words turn to curses. Modestly dressed women strip layers and bounce their finest assets to hooting men through open windows.

Moryana leading us, we emerge from the birch wood. Our name is upon a hundred tongues.

Rusalka.

Rusalka.

Rusalka.

They joke openly about our fine figures, debate our origins and intent. The crowd flows like a rushing river passed merchant shops, now closed. The air is sharp with the scent of mead and human stink. Near every hand holds a glass or goblet. Near every beard is white with foam, every tooth stained dark with wine. The needling desire for violence deepens as we follow the crowd.

They wind through cobblestone alleys, and when the road disappears into a meadow of long grasses, they continue. The heavens are a bruise of blood-red and navy. Women remove their shoes, leave them in a long line of stinking leather. At the meadow's center roars a bonfire. A spindly man, bandana tied around his head, plucks a lyre. Drums beat from every side, struck by calloused hands. An elderly woman, gray hair wiry and free sings baritone over the melody of a girl, not more than fifteen. They sing of fertile fields and full wombs, of blessed crops and new babies.

"They sing folly," a dark-eyed woman tells her partner. "The Rusalki seek only revenge. To take life, not to grant it."

Yinka sits upon an overturned tree some distance back. I keep an eye on her as Lily settles cross-legged in the soft grasses. She unravels the bun I twisted, yanks my hair into three sections and braids it roughly. We catch the eye of a salt-and-pepper-haired man. He clutches a moldy bit of bread, which I suppose to be his offering. Lily leans close to his ear.

"Might you help us, good sir?"

He looks me head to toe, then Lily the same. "It would be my life's honor, good women, to help such fine ladies as yourselves."

Lily draws a circle with her fingertip upon his earlobe. "We seek our cousin, Edward Dempsey, of London. Might you tell us where we could find him?"

His forehead wrinkles. "Of London, eh? We've a Dempsey, yes. Lives up the hill on Briar St. I don't know he hails from London yet—"

"Thank you." My body clenches as she says it. He knows not what he has gifted her, and yet I do. It is my end. The end for Lily and I.

Moryana, Dana, and Dalia circle the festivities like birds of prey. When the townspeople begin to dance in circles around the fire, they join them. Darkness penetrates the sky and the fire roars ever higher as dancing men toss offerings to us into the blaze.

"Spare me, Rusalka!"

"Bless my fields."

"May the rye harvest be abundant."

With hunched shoulders, a woman slips between dancers, jostled by their feverish movement along the way. Sadness hovers around her like a shadow. Her offering is small, a doll wound of twine. Though her accent is strong, I hear her quiet words as she casts the doll into the fire.

"Please, Rusalki. A child. You are my last hope." Flames bounce off the tears in her eyes, and she squeezes her lids shut. Yinka's stare is upon her as she winds her way through the merriment to a quiet spot behind the crowd. I turn from the festivities, Lily engrossed in flirtation with a fisherman and his wife, and watch as Yinka approaches the pleading woman.

Through the singing and drumbeats, I don't hear the words they exchange, but watch the movement of my sister's lips. Yinka presses a hand to her belly, and I'm drawn to them. As I move closer, I catch bits of their conversation.

"Not one, but two you shall have."

The woman grasps her own belly. "I feel them!" Tears stream freely down her cheeks. "Thank you!" She collapses onto the floor, weeping with relief. For the first time, a smile crosses Yinka's lips.

"Though I desire not to take life," she says, "I find within myself the ability to give it."

It may be a trick of the eyes, but I think her flesh takes on a greenish hue.

"Though just this one time." A tear streaks her cheek as well, and a rustling behind her draws my attention to the tree line. A flash of red hair, and a boyish, freckled face peeks through the brush. He reaches out a hand. I turn Yinka toward him with a gentle nudge to her shoulder.

She gasps.

Arms outstretched, she runs to him, and when he wraps his arms around her, their figures become thin as wind, until I stare only at the birch wood, leaves of yellow and green.

The night grows old and the crowd thins. All have retired to their homes, the fire dwindled down to embers.

Pale sky tells us morning is near, and only four men remain, tumbling into one another with their drunkenness as they attempt a sloppy dance. My sisters grow impatient. Lily approaches a sunburnt man with thinning hair and invites him to dance.

"I've no notes for you, whore!"

The others erupt into laughter. "Good then, that your money is not my aim," she says.

He swallows and places his grimy hand in hers. Her hand upon his hip, she moves slowly back and forth and he mirrors her movements, sliding his hand from her torso to her buttocks. Lily only grins and sways faster.

Moryana, Dalia, and Dana, as if on cue, summon the others. Pair by pair they circle the fire, swaying this way and that. Drunken hands grope and tug at their linens, but none pay it any mind. Lily invites her man to a girlish spin, and he complies, his cheeks flushing with shame after realizing he has done so.

The others do the same in turn.

Dalia begins to sing. A chanting song with plodding rhythm. The steps of the men match it in time, and their faces suggest bewilderment at the movement, as if their limbs are affixed to invisible strings. Moryana joins the chorus, but not with words. Clicking sounds leave her throat in a dizzying pattern. And while the men's feet match Dalia's beat, their arms strike the air in time with Moryana's clicks.

Dana claps.

Slowly, at first, the pace of a heartbeat.

Sweat rolls from the men's faces. They blink it away as it rolls into their eyes.

Dana claps faster.

With each smack of her hands, the men spin a tight circle.

My sisters step from the feverish dance, Dalia still singing, Moryana still clicking, and Dana clapping faster and faster. The men move closer and closer to the dying fire, stepping into the coals as they spin, sending sparks flittering into the waning darkness.

Another voice joins in. High and clear and in perfect time.

Dance, we dance!
Round the fire you go
Dance for we Rusalki

The tone is strange, but the hum of my throat tells me the voice is my own. The cloying pain of need erupts into a second verse.

You call for we
From land to sea
Now dance for we Rusalki

Sweat stains the men's clothing. One cries out, then another. Anguish upon their faces, they collapse in time with a last, forceful clap from Dana. Silence falls upon my sisters and I, only the faint crackling of fire meets our ears. We draw upon them like vultures, flies already circling their vacant, gaping eyes. The familiar trance comes for each of us; hands turned to blades, we consume their exploded hearts. So hungry are we, that not a bit of their rusty innards is wasted. As if by some magic of Green Week, not a drop of them stains our immaculate finery. Licking the blood from our lips, we appear as we ever have. Lovely and terrible, pictures of perfect beauty. Though perhaps, a bit green. Reduced to pieces, we toss their clean bones into the smoldering pit.

A fine, final meal.

Chapter Fifteen

My husband lives in a simple stone cottage, hugged on all sides by vibrant ferns and flowering vines. Soft upon our feet, the dirt walkway is free from weeds and curves around a mosaic birdbath.

"It's odd, isn't it?" I ask.

Lily would prefer to pay me no mind. Her focus in singular.

"I never knew him to be so fastidious with gardening."

"Hah! You think he has not taken another wife?" She *tsks* me. "Ever the optimist."

The brass door knocker clangs against an arched wooden door. I rise to my tiptoes to peek through the circular window, but the reflection of sun off the glass makes it impossible to see through. I pick at hanging skin around my thumbnail as we wait.

"Do you suppose he will remember us?" Lily's smirk has a feral quality.

I allow the question to go unanswered.

"I believe he shall." She turns back to the door just as it begins to glide open. In the doorway is the face of a young man, perhaps aged twenty. There's a familiar air about him, his strong jawline and bushy brows, but he is most certainly not my husband.

"We are looking for a cousin of ours," Lily says, bouncing on the balls of her feet. "Edward Dempsey. Is he some relation of yours?"

The man's tanned face relaxes into a smile. "So you have found me!" He waves us in with a jovial flip of his hand. "Please, do come in. And merry Green Week!"

I follow Lily over the threshold, and the cottage smells of baking bread. There's not a dust bunny in sight. Books are stacked in neat rows across perfectly straight shelves, a plush teal couch is centered across from a hearth, an indigo blanket neatly folded over its arm. I see no empty bottles of liquor, just a tidy but threadbare rug. My husband could not live here.

"Edward is a strong name, to be sure," I say as the man pours us each a glass of lemonade. "But my cousin is somewhat older than you, sir. Is there, perhaps, someone else in town by the name Dempsey?"

He passes us each a glass, and Lily's eyes remain fixed on him as she tilts it back to take a drink.

"I am the only Dempsey in town, to my knowledge."

Feeling strangely at ease in the man's presence, I settle myself upon the couch, velveteen fabric soft against my skin.

"I'm most sorry to disappoint. Dempsey is a most common name, though not in this part of the world, I must admit. Perhaps your cousin settled elsewhere?"

My eyes drift over the hearth where a portrait hangs. "Oil paint?"

"Aye," he says, taking quick steps to cross the room. He inspects it closely. "I spent a full year on this one, though, I'm afraid I did her no justice."

"Your wife?" Lily stands back at a distance, the menace on her mind visible even through her placid words and coy smile.

"No, my—"

As the word prepares to leave his lips, *before* sinks its talons into me once more. It comes in rapid flashes, filling in decades of my life in radiant images, all at once.

Lily and I, but children, clad in pastel dresses, flowers in our hair, dancing in circles in a field.

A passenger ship. Our journey from England. My arm linked in Edward's while Lily—now a young woman—glares at me from behind, twirling an umbrella balanced on the crook of her neck.

A baby. Delivered in the same room where Edward found us that day. Wailing and covered in blood. *I'll name him Edward, after his father,* I'd said. And my husband was pleased.

"Mother."

As sure as I know it myself, I know Lily has learned the same truths. Though while my body fills with longing to reach for my child, to tell him I am here, at last, Lily sucks her teeth.

"And what of your father?"

My son places my portrait back in its spot on the hearth. It's not altogether my likeness, but so young he was when I—

"I'm afraid he passed away many years back. He reveled in too much drink."

"Hmmm." Lily nods as she considers.

Edward Jr. tosses his hands into the air. "How rude of me! Pouring out my life's story and not a single question of my distant relations, traveled long and far to visit, only to find that their cousin—"

"Died." Lily makes no pretense about it, and Edward Jr. stills.

"I—I'm sorry. I did not intend to deliver such sensitive news." His head tips in a respectful nod.

"Sorry indeed," Lily's voice is low, but not too low for him to hear.

"Tell me," he goes on, now with a suspicious air. "What compelled you to seek him out? Pardon my assumption, but with many years since his passing, you must not have been terribly close. Do you require assistance of some kind? Perhaps I might be of aid. I have guest rooms, if you'd like. It would be no trouble at all—"

"You are right to offer yourself as his replacement." Lily advances upon him, and I rise from my seat.

"Lily, I think we should speak in private."

Her hand silences me. "You are right. We have traveled far. Only to find disappointment. Though perhaps," she looks to me, "not a total one."

I cock my head, urging her to step back, but she pushes me instead. A hard blow to the center of my chest topples me over, sending my hidden ship in a bottle rolling across the stone floor. When I regain myself, she's lifted him by the neck, his face already scarlet and plastered with shock.

"Lily, stop!" I return to my feet. "He's done nothing. This is not the vengeance we seek."

"And yet"—she tightens her grip—"it is the one available to us."

My child makes a sputtering sound, and Lily's hair has taken on a greenish hue. Seconds tick by, counted by a grandfather clock that now seems to echo and reverberate off the walls, seconds as long and short as those moments in the tidepool, when a child's eyes passed over the body of his mother.

Edward Jr. turns a darker shade.

I must do something.

I crouch. I know not what becomes me, but I sprint at Lily, making hard contact with her body such that she drops Edward Jr. and lands on the floor, my body atop hers.

"You wench!" Her arm lashes out to strike me, but I catch it, pin both her wrists to the floor.

"You will not do this. I love you, but I will not let you do this."

She writhes beneath me as Edward Jr. takes sucking breaths on the floor beside us.

"You would defend this man? You would place your hands upon me?"

It's a stab in my chest, her insinuation of betrayal. "And yet you wonder why I would never settle for you. Well here's why! You needn't ask yourself any longer. This is your *true* nature, and I've seen it all along, even when we were children."

A sleeping rage wakes. "And yet you followed me from the shores of England! Made a home just down the street from mine. Why, Lily? To dangle yourself in front of me for your amusement?"

"For my amusement, yes!" She spits the words at me. They crash into every illusion I've ever held about our love.

A hairline fracture in the image of us spirals outward, like a snaking break in a sheet of ice.

I lean close. Press my body into hers. "You love me," I hiss. "The best you know how—which is to say not well!—yet, you love me. More than anyone else in this world or the next. Lesser only to the way you love yourself, which I've always known would remain unmatched."

Her smile widens. A cramped giggle morphs to rapturous laughter. "So you know me after all."

Quieting footsteps draw my attention to the open door. Edward Jr. has run into the garden. I hold Lily in place until I'm sure she'll be unable to give chase. "I have always known you, and shamefully, I love you still." When I ease my body off her, she stretches before sitting up, as if we've just concluded a session of love-making.

"I will find him." She yawns, as if the entire escapade now bores her. My body vibrates. Lily will never choose me. In a daze, I cross the room, retrieve my glass bottle full of insect sailors. I clutch it to my breast, and in that moment, a whisper. It's tiny, as if from the throat of a wasp, or the ghost of a snake, or a pair of ill-fated twins. It speaks words in a language foreign to me, and yet the sound is so lovely I cannot help but repeat them in my mind. I roll them over, again and again, bottle pressed to me tight, the other hand clutching the dragon's teeth with such force I think they might bite me from beyond the grave.

If Lily comments, I do not hear it. I whisper this prayer, or spell, or blessing, and all the pain and lust and loneliness of my life, of *after* and *before* culminates into swirling color. I'm lifted, or perhaps just have the strange sense of being lifted, and my sense of the world around me collapses.

I go cold.

When I wake, Scylla's sails billow overhead. The deck is quiet.

How did I get here?

There's a rustling behind me and I turn to find Lily's crumpled form, waking as if from a long sleep. I crouch beside her, pushing strands of hair from her face. She stares up, a look of bewilderment. I follow her gaze to find the most unusual sky. It has taken on something of a mirror surface.

"Is this our rest?"

Lily stumbles to her feet, crossing the deck to the port side. The translucent shine is all around us, mirrored where light refracts. Male voices drift up from the sleeping chambers below. And it hits me, all at once.

I take Lily's hand, guide her to our familiar stairs which lead below deck. There we find my sailors, who cower before us and slink off to their rooms. Our room sits empty, bed made, as if waiting.

"I don't understand." Lily has the innocent look of a child. "Who are those sailors? Where is Lucinda? Our sisters?"

A great force rocks our tiny Scylla, and I run to the porthole window. Squinting, I am met not with sky, but by the warped image of my grown child's living room through layers of glass. Edward Jr. has lifted us, inspects my ship in a bottle. Whether he knows we dwell inside, I know not. But he places us upon his mantle with care and angles it so I've a view of my portrait.

I gaze upon the painted rendering of my face, his memory of my face. "Endless present."

Lily is my echo. "Endless present." She laces her fingers through mine. Her lavender scent fills the room.

"My captain," she says, reaching over my shoulder to caress my cheek from behind, equal parts relenting and menacing. "For now."

And all we have is now. This thought swirls and strengthens me. Just as strange words etch themselves into the corners of my mind, I grow powerful with knowledge. Knowledge of the ritual to release us, should I like.

But I shall not.

Lily has eluded me, in more than one life. Danced just beyond my reach for her titillation and amusement. Greatly I have suffered in pursuit of her. Rapturously she delighted in my anguish. But no more. For the old gods have witnessed my trials, have granted the longing of my heart. No more distractions. No more games. Together we shall be, ad infinitum, bound by an inversion of love and a thick wall of glass.

ABOUT THE AUTHOR

Rae Knowles (she/her) is a queer woman whose debut novel, *The Stradivarius*, released May 2023 and hit #1 in Amazon's LGBTQ+ Horror and Thriller categories. Her collaboration with April Yates, *Lies That Bind*, is due out in early '24. A number of her short stories have been featured in publications like *Dark Matter Ink*, *Nightmare*, *Seize the Press*, *Taco Bell Quarterly*, and *Nosetouch Press*. She is editor-in-chief of Lady Mantis Books, an imprint of Brigids Gate Press.

You can find recent updates on her work at RaeKnowles.com and follow her on Twitter @_Rae_Knowles.

ACKNOWLEDGEMENTS

The creation of this book is largely due to the love and support of my wife. Thank you for the sacrifices you've made so I can lock myself in the office to write. Thank you to my parents for buying every story I've ever published, and to my son for being so understanding when I can't play because I have to work on a story.

My sincerest thanks to Grace R. Reynolds for her help with the Russian translations, and to my early readers Michelle Cruz, Evelyn Freeling, Dana Vickerson, Zachary Rosenberg, Brett Mitchell Kent, Katrina Carruth, The Coven, and C.S. Humble for providing vital feedback.

None of my work would be possible without a strong writing community. I'm not able to name you all, but you know you who are, and I deeply thank you.

CONTENT WARNINGS

Gore, ritualistic animal harm, sexual content, murder, violence against women

More from Brigids Gate Press

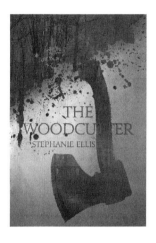

A tragic accident, shrouded in mystery, leads to a family reunion in the hidden village of Little Hatchet, located in the smothering shadow of GodBeGone Wood, the home of the mythical Woodcutter and Grandma. Alec Eades rediscovers his bond with GodBeGone Wood and the future his father agreed to years ago as nefarious landowner Oliver Hayward schemes to raise money for the village by re-enacting part of the Woodcutter legend. Old wounds are re-opened and ties of blood and friendship are tested to the extreme when the Woodcutter is summoned and Grandma returns.

Ten-year-old Hannah has Down syndrome and oodles of courage, but should she trust the alluring tree creature who smells of Mamma's perfume or the blue-eyed wolf who warns her not to enter the woods under any circumstances?

When Hannah and her doting father move to Wales following her parents' divorce, Hannah finds herself faced with many challenges—a new school, new friends, a place at the local drama club. At first she rises to the challenge, but when her mother, a famous actor, moves to Sweden on a permanent basis leaving Hannah with nothing more than a trunk of old theatre costumes as a parting gift, things take a turn for the worse.

The Wolf and the Favour is a tale of love, trust, and courage. A tale that champions the neurodivergent voice and proves the true power of a person's strength lies within themselves.

Set in 1926, nine-year-old Rosalyn invents a new game to play with the girls she shares a dormitory with in the Hawthorne House Orphanage. Revolving around a Royal Court, their make-believe game quickly becomes a way to gain some measure of control in their unhappy lives. But when the rules start changing and the stakes start rising, nothing is safe, and Rosalyn finds that she's willing to get her hands dirty in order to be the Queen.

The story of a girl begins with a boy. On Christmas morning, 1982, nine-year-old Jude Bendz survives the shocking and mysterious death of his twin sister, Mary. Bewildered by grief, he is comforted when, miraculously, Mary's ghost appears, her spirit quickly informing a series of fantastic apparitions through which her life—and death—come into clearer focus. Problems soon arise, however, when his sister, promising salvation, places him at the center of a wide, yet narrowing plot that increasingly puts his life in mortal danger.

A novel that transcends its historical moment, *Being Dead* brilliantly subverts the conventions of the traditional Ghost story. Reconstructing her own death through a series of spooky visitations and cryptic clues that, in time, seem to assume the shape of formal challenges, Mary creates for Jude a blueprint that blurs the line between truth and revenge, love and hate, an account that threatens to shatter their family's perfect image.

Luminous, evocative, and set amidst the decline of American exceptionalism and the nuclear family, this is at once an enthralling adventure, a stirring love story, and a work of striking power in the face of stark solitude. As Mary interweaves elements of a set past that portends a harrowing future, life rears up large and ripples against death's certain pressures, generating mesmerizing suspense and surprising empathy. Yielding poignant insights into the nature of love and loss, savagery and splendor, *Being Dead* asserts itself as a new American gothic—hugely powerful, majestically unassuming, and keenly unsettling.

Visit our website at: www.brigidsgatepress.com

Made in the USA
Columbia, SC
10 November 2024

45810240R00086